JENNY'S STAR

Jenny Knight, director of the Cherry Valley Retirement Home, works hard to make her residents happy. But this Christmas it's difficult pretending to be joyful. Still smarting over a failed romance, Jenny just wants Christmas to be over. It gets no easier when Parker McAllister, the son of one of her residents, turns up — toting an enormous tree, and intent on spreading good cheer. Parker finds her ravishing, and despite her resistance, shows her how special the season can be. And, as Jenny's defences melt away, she knows what she wants for Christmas — to win this wonderful man's heart!

Books by Patricia Werner
Published by The House of Ulverscroft:

THE WILL
PRAIRIE FIRE
IF TRUTH BE KNOWN

PATRICIA WERNER

◆

JENNY'S STAR

Complete and Unabridged

ULVERSCROFT
Leicester

First published in the
United States of America in 1999

First Large Print Edition
published 2008

British Library CIP Data

Werner, Patricia
  Jenny's star.—Large print ed.—
  Ulverscroft large print series: romance
  1. Love stories
  2. Large type books
  I. Title
  813.5'4 [F]

  ISBN 978–1–84782–217–8

Published by
F. A. Thorpe (Publishing)
Anstey, Leicestershire

Set by Words & Graphics Ltd.
Anstey, Leicestershire
Printed and bound in Great Britain by
T. J. International Ltd., Padstow, Cornwall

This book is printed on acid-free paper

Acknowledgements

Many thanks to my helpful friends who contributed to this plot: Marianne G. Rucker, Maxwell Rucker, Alice Kober, Carla Gertner, Joyce Sullivan, Jeffrey Agrell, Sylvie Kurtz and Kelsey Roberts. This book is dedicated to your spirit of play.

1

'It's only for two weeks, Jenn,' Maureen West assured her sister, Jenny Knight.

Jenny stood, clipboard under her tweed-suited arm in the covered unloading area in front of the Cherry Valley Retirement Home. It was the Friday afternoon of a long week.

Maureen unloaded the large, soft, black leather case from her green Subaru station wagon. She lugged the case to the tiled entryway while Jenny stared, mouth open in protest.

'Roger can't have his tuba here,' she objected.

But her sister was hardly listening. She set the case down and returned to the car. Her denim-covered backside was all that was visible now, for her head and upper body were thrust into the backseat of the car as she retrieved more luggage.

Maureen came up for air once more, auburn, wavy hair blowing around her face. In the typically sunny Denver weather, Maureen wore only a denim jacket over her slightly plump figure. November had proved to be a true Indian summer, and they'd not seen any snow except for some light flakes six weeks earlier. Thanksgiving weekend was just past, and Jenny was beginning to grapple with the extra festivities the holiday season would add to her already stressful job.

She had been general manager of the Cherry Valley Retirement Home since September, and she only had another month to save the place from closing its doors. Now, with its painful reminders, the Christmas season was doubly hard to get through. But to have her nephew Roger dumped on her doorstep in addition to everything else was unthinkable.

'Why aren't you taking Roger with you?' she demanded of her sister, watching the eleven-year-old nephew in question extract himself from the opposite side of the station wagon.

And why isn't he carrying any of his own bags? she wondered silently. Is this why men were such arrogant, self-centered creatures? Did they all have mothers who hauled and lifted and carried the precious child's belongings everywhere when they were young, as if they were superior beings? But she held her tongue. Maureen did not appreciate advice on child-rearing any more than Jenny appreciated Maureen's advice about the way she ran her life.

'Roger has school,' said Maureen in answer to Jenny's question.

She gave a sigh that said Jenny should know that. 'If he goes with us to Maine, he won't have anything to do. John's aunt's stroke has caused enough havoc. He only has two weeks off from work to get Aunt Bea settled in a new facility. You've got to help us, Jenn. I'm at my wit's end.'

Jenny lifted a reddish-brown eyebrow and frowned down her slim nose at her shorter, plumper sister. She spoke in a softer tone, not wanting Roger to hear them arguing about him.

'I'm at my own wit's end as well, sister dear. With the extra holiday work, I don't see how I'll have time for Roger. I've told you that the corporate office is sending someone out for inspection in two weeks. What do you expect me to do?'

Roger remained in the circular drive behind the car, hands in the pockets of his baggy trousers, oversized sweatshirt drooping off one skinny shoulder. Brown eyes peered through his brown, plastic-framed glasses under callow brows and light brown, medium-length hair, parted in the middle and clipped to ear length. He had wandered along the sidewalk and was examining the bushes and grounds of the front of the brick

3

establishment, as if deciding whether it would suit him.

Maureen didn't argue. Instead, she just turned on the charm, her golden-brown eyes pleading.

'Jenny, dear. It won't really be that bad. The school bus will pick him up and drop him off here; I checked. All you have to do is make sure he does his homework and practices his tuba. His music lessons are Saturday at ten.'

'I'm just not a parent, that's all,' Jenny hissed. 'I . . . I'm just afraid he won't be happy with me. I don't have time to entertain a kid right now.'

But her arguments fell on deaf ears. Maureen gave her a hug, honey melting her words.

'Don't you worry. Roger won't be any trouble. He can entertain himself.'

Maureen turned to shield her eyes from the bright sun. 'Roger, come on. Help Jenny carry your things inside.'

Roger cocked his head and looked up suspiciously at Jenny, pursing his lips and then scrunching them sideways. Then he dropped his gaze, shrugged one shoulder and shuffled over to place a hand on the handle of the large tuba case.

'Where are we going?'

Jenny lifted her hands in exasperated surrender. She could see she didn't really have a choice. Maureen's husband's Aunt Bea needed to be moved into a facility in faraway Maine. If Roger had to stay in school, she guessed she was stuck. He'd just better be as self-contained as her sister made it sound. But she'd known Roger West for all of his eleven years, and she had her doubts.

'Well, I guess it has to be this way,' she told Maureen on an exasperated breath.

Maureen gave a few last-minute instructions to her son and dropped a kiss on his head. Then she closed all the car doors except the one on the driver's side.

'Got to run, Jenn. There's still a bunch to do. Thanks. I'll call you when we get there.'

With that, the auburn-haired tornado climbed into her car and drove away. Jenny was left with her eleven-year-old nephew, some luggage and a tuba. She sighed and reached for a suitcase.

'If you can carry that,' she said, pointing to the big black case, 'I'll get these.'

Jenny's apartment was adjacent to the retirement center on the other side of the building. The easiest way to get there was to wind through the halls of the main building in front of them. The east wing would bring them out to a courtyard, across which was a smaller building with a few apartments.

'We'll go through here,' she told Roger. 'It's faster than going around the outside and down the hill. Especially with all this stuff.'

She lifted her clipboard and flipped to one of the pages listing the equipment available in the facility.

'I might be able to sign out a housekeeping cart from the supply room. There's no way we can carry everything that far.'

Roger shrugged. 'Okay.'

The outer doors to the elegant lobby slid open as they approached. Grace Douglas, the program director for the facility, looked up at them from the circular counter of the front desk. Grace was an exuberant, angular woman of thirty-five, with short, wavy, practical brown hair. Her generous mouth, green eyes and wide cheekbones always displayed vivid interest in everything around her. As program director, she had the efficiency of a drill sergeant, the tactics of a Sherman tank and the heart of a pussycat. And with her forthright and direct manner, she was incredibly good at her job, constantly pumping up the elderly residents and organizing them into this activity and that. She leaned over the counter to look at Roger and gave him a big smile.

'A little young to be moving in here, aren't

you?' she said in her direct, teasing voice.

'This is my nephew,' said Jenny, barely stifling a weary sigh. 'My sister has taken off for Maine to help her husband's aunt move. Roger will be a guest for two weeks. Roger, say hello to Grace Douglas. Grace is our program and activity director.'

'Hello.' The round, speculative brown eyes assessed the tall, athletic woman.

'Hello, Roger. Nice to have you. What's in that case?'

'My tuba,' said Roger, standing straighter. 'I play in the band.'

'Oh,' said Grace, getting really interested now. 'You'll have to tell me about your band,' she said. 'We're always looking for groups to come and entertain.'

She waved them on. 'See you later.'

Jenny was still trying to manhandle the luggage off to one side of the lobby when she saw the other woman's head crane toward the doors behind them. Grace's eyebrows lifted into brown arches, and her green eyes lit up with that predatory look of hers, and she hurried around the desk. Jenny glanced back to see the cause of Grace's interest.

A tall, broad-shouldered man with striking presence strode into the lobby. Thick brown hair and wide cheek-bones complemented a self-assured, straight nose and brown eyes

7

fringed with dark, thick lashes. As he came nearer, he located Grace, and his full, attractive lips curved into a polite smile.

'Mr. McAllister,' chimed Grace's megaphone voice, 'I see you have our tree.'

Jenny looked beyond him and saw through the double set of glass doors that a large Christmas tree stuck out of the end of a red pickup truck. *Oh, of course, the tree.* Grace had told her about it. They were saving money by having the son of one of the residents donate it.

Seeing Jenny still standing there, Grace performed her duties.

'Jenny Knight, this is Parker McAllister. Parker was kind enough to donate our Christmas tree.'

'Thank you,' said Jenny, extending her hand. 'We appreciate it.'

His grip was warm and firm, his masculine charm the kind that sends chills along a woman's arm. She recognized the bump-de-bump of her heart for what it was: a response to his magnetic charm. It threw her off balance for a moment, but she clenched her jaw.

Her mind scrambled to remember the exact connection as Parker McAllister smiled at her, causing warning bells to go off in her head.

'Miss Knight,' said Parker. 'My mother has spoken of you.'

Right! Jenny finally realized. His mother was Dorothy McAllister. She eased her lips into a smile.

'Your mother is very sweet. We enjoy having her here.'

She tried to sound convincing. She'd only been at Cherry Valley Retirement Center for three months. That was a short time to put all the names and faces together, especially when her primary duty was to turn the fiscally teetering place around. But she'd been here long enough to become aware of who was who in the coffee klatches.

The job had come along at a time when she'd needed to throw herself into something anyway. The fact that her grandmother had lived here happily until her death a few years earlier had made it a personal mission. Cherry Valley was losing money. If she didn't turn things around for them, they would have to close the doors. Granny wouldn't have liked that.

So, after a disappointing relationship with a man who had been less than he seemed, she'd just taken herself and her MBA and landed the job running this place. Mr. Ex couldn't accuse her of being selfish now.

She was still smiling icily at the handsome

9

hunk in front of her. After her debacle with Drake, she wanted no more truck with handsome hunks. This one had let his handshake linger while his eyes held hers. Oh, those gorgeous long eyelashes, she thought, getting side-tracked again. Just the sort of thing to throw a woman off course. He probably knew how to use them well.

She cleared her throat. 'Can we get someone to help you with the tree?' she asked.

His smile broadened, and she could swear she saw an actual twinkle come into his deep brown eyes.

'Why, yes. If you have a strong young man about, he could carry one end.'

'I'll help.'

Jenny turned in surprise. She'd completely forgotten Roger, and she didn't think Parker had quite so young a man in mind when he'd asked for help.

'That's all right, Roger,' said Jenny. 'We can get one of the waiters or maintenance men to do it.'

She looked back at Parker. 'This is my nephew, come to stay for a couple of weeks.'

'Great.' He smiled broadly at the boy. 'Well, Roger, if you don't mind some pine needles in your face, you can give me a hand.'

Jenny was left standing with her mouth

open in the middle of the lobby, next to a round glass table with a ceramic fountain on it as Parker and Roger nonchalantly moved through the double set of glass doors to the truck. Finally she shut her mouth.

'They'll never be able to do it themselves,' she told Grace, who had come out from behind the desk.

'I wouldn't be so sure about that,' said Grace with rising interest. 'I'd think a man like that could do *anything*. Maybe we can keep him around here for a while.'

She made a purring growl in her throat. 'You don't see specimens like that walk in here every day.'

Jenny had grown used to Grace's unsubtle ways of expressing herself. She watched Parker's easy movements with cynical suspicion. Grace was obviously appreciating the sight of his long, muscular legs and trim hips in tan cords, moving around the truck and climbing into the back. The black turtleneck he wore enhanced his broad chest. She could imagine abs of steel beneath the soft material of his shirt. Just the sort of man to beware of. Full of themselves, sure of their appeal to women, were men like that. Drake had been one of them, and she'd learned the hard way how dangerous it was to get swept off one's feet by a 'sexy male specimen,' as Grace put

11

it. It also wasted a lot of precious time.

She drew in a breath and straightened her shoulders. If Grace wanted to gawk, that was her business. Jenny had more important things to do.

From inside the back of the pickup, Parker eased the tree out so that Roger could hold the lighter end. Soon the boy's head was lost among the branches. At least his glasses would protect his eyes, Jenny thought. Then Parker slid over the tailgate and hefted the bottom of the tree to his shoulders, careful not to damage any of the branches.

'It does look like a very nice tree,' Jenny said. 'Where did he get it?'

'He sells them.'

'He sells Christmas trees?' Jenny opened her eyes wide in surprise. Somehow the cut of his clothes and his manicured nails had made her think he was an executive of some company or a rich playboy.

Grace nodded, speaking confidentially. 'The way I heard it, he was VP of marketing for an electronics company that merged.' She rolled her green eyes. 'He was downsized. Mutual parting of the ways, so I hear.'

'To a Christmas tree lot?'

Jenny realized that she was in danger of sounding repetitive and lacking in poise. But her whirlwind sister had knocked some of her control right out the door this afternoon. She hadn't quite recovered from having the role of baby-sitter thrust upon her for the holiday season. She still wanted to spit lightning bolts of annoyance about that. It couldn't be a more inconvenient time. Still, Grace's comment made her curious. If this man had just lost his job, how could he afford to keep his mother in this upscale retirement home?

'Oh, look out,' Jenny cried.

She came to her senses just in time to prevent Roger from aiming the point of the Christmas tree right at the sculptured fountain on the circular glass table in the lobby. She stuck out an arm and steered him to the side while realizing with horror that she'd failed to ask any of the residents to step aside for the tree coming through.

'Can you wait a second?' she called to Parker over her shoulder. 'I need to make some room for you.'

Her steely grip on Roger's thin shoulders brought him to a halt. 'Wait here,' she said to him before she let go.

'Mrs. Seymour, Mr. Mossback,' she called sweetly to two of the elderly residents watching the proceedings from the junction of the lobby and the pathway to the parlor area. She tried to regain her professional, patient manner.

'Would you mind waiting over here, please? We need to bring the tree through. We're taking it over there next to the fireplace.'

The elderly pair peered at the tree.

'Oh, how nice,' said Mrs. Johnson. 'Certainly we'll move.'

Jenny waited until the path was clear and then signaled for one of the uniformed nurse's aides to move some of the other residents out of the way, as well. Then she breathed again. A big part of working in a retirement home was just making sure people didn't collide with each other. The fast pace of the staff and visitors could only too easily precipitate near accidents with the slower-paced, older residents, ambling on canes and walkers.

'Okay,' said Jenny, marching back to the waiting tree. 'All clear. But please move slowly. There are some chairs and lamps to negotiate.'

'Lead the way, General,' said Parker.

His handsome head leaned out from among the branches.

She steered Roger carefully. A few steps more and they made it to the parlor area, where a Christmas-tree stand waited next to the gas fireplace in the middle of the room. The brick fireplace was open on both sides. Beyond that, floor-to-ceiling glass windows opened to a redwood deck. The deck overlooked a courtyard backed by a grove of apple trees, stretching to a green belt behind the complex. An ideal setting for a Christmas tree, the center of social events on this floor.

Parker maneuvered the tree into the stand, finally lifting the lighter end off Roger's shoulders. Jenny stood back. The tree was full and lovely, obviously a top pick from the lot.

'It's lovely,' Jenny told him as he brushed off his hands. 'I'm sure the residents will enjoy decorating it.'

He folded his six-foot frame down to the floor to secure the stand. A pro, Jenny thought. But then, Christmas trees were his business. She exchanged a quick look with Grace, whose eyebrows were raised in open speculation. Then Grace moved away to take care of some other business and chat with the residents who had come to see the tree. Roger wandered over to the windows to look out at the deck, a few pine needles still entwined with his hair.

When Parker regained his height, Jenny thanked him again, not liking the fact that her pulse still tingled. A bad sign.

'I, um, appreciate the tree. Do you need a receipt for the donation? For your tax deduction, I mean.'

She flushed. It seemed embarrassing to mention his tax situation on the heels of learning that he'd just been laid off. Of course, that was silly. His affairs were none of her business.

Parker brushed off his hands and grinned. 'Sure, I'll take a receipt if you have one.'

She was about to tell him to step into her office when she remembered Roger. The air went out of her lungs. She would have to take care of that responsibility first.

'I'll ask Grace to give you the receipt. I'm afraid I was just escorting my nephew to my apartment.'

'That his luggage back there in the lobby?' asked Parker. His deep voice hummed with casual confidence.

'Well, yes. We were going to get a cart to carry it.'

Parker's eyes twinkled again. 'Why don't you let me help you? If it's very far, we can throw the luggage in my pickup.'

'Oh, well, you probably need to get back to work,' she said.

Another grin from the handsome face. 'My assistant is handling things at the lot.'

She didn't see how she could gracefully refuse.

'Well, in that case. Roger,' she called to her nephew. 'The gentleman is going to take the luggage to the apartment. You can ride with him.'

'The quarters in the front of the pickup are close,' said Parker. 'But we'll fit three in easily enough.'

'Oh, that's all right. I can walk.'

The thought of close quarters with such a devastatingly handsome man did something to Jenny's blood, setting off alarm bells again. He was probably aware of his attractiveness, and she took pains to keep her distance.

'Don't you want to show us the way?' Parker asked gently.

'Oh, well, I guess I'd better.'

No choice, then, unless she insisted on walking around the building, followed by a pickup going at five miles per hour. That would look ridiculous.

Roger dragged himself away from the windows and followed dutifully along. In the lobby, Parker picked up the tuba case and one of the suitcases with ease and strode out to the truck. When he came back for the second bag, they followed him outside.

'Pretty cool,' said Roger as he climbed into the high front seat.

Jenny's business suit wasn't designed to give her the freedom of movement to comfortably clamber into the seat, but she hauled herself up. Once there, she tried to smooth her skirt down over her legs. But as Parker came around to shut her door, his glance grazed off her knees. He shut the door, giving her a place to rest her arm. Roger continued to wriggle and stare at the dashboard, plying Parker with questions about the truck as they started up.

'How many cylinders does it have?' asked Roger.

'Eight,' said Parker. 'And it's four-wheel drive.'

'Wow. Can you drive it off the road?'

'Sure,' answered Parker with a grin. 'I go off road all the time in the mountains.'

'Wow,' Roger exclaimed again.

Jenny directed him around the building to the back parking lot. At the far end of the east wing, the parking lot was shared by a low, two-story building with small balconies.

'You can pull up at that side door,' she said.

She struggled with her skirt again as Parker got out and helped her down.

'Uh, thanks,' she said. Parker got the bags out from the back.

'No problem.' His smile disarmed her again. 'I'll carry them on in if you can get the doors.'

This time she wasn't going to let Roger think he was being waited on by a servant.

'Roger, please carry the smaller bag while I open the door.'

The boy shrugged and picked up the bag. They all trooped through the glass door and down the carpeted hallway to the elevator. On the second floor, the little procession was repeated until they came to her door. Then she unlocked her apartment and led them through.

Jenny's second-floor apartment was decorated in warm beiges and greens. A red-brick fireplace stood next to French doors leading to a small balcony that wrapped around the corner. In the living room, brass lamps sat on corner tables and on top of her entertainment center. An open counter separated a small dining area from the kitchen.

'The guest room's through here.' She pointed to the short hallway leading toward the bedrooms and bathroom.

Parker carried the tuba case and suitcase into the small spare room, made smaller by his large presence, the bags and Roger squeezing in behind them.

'This will be your room,' Jenny told Roger.

'Where's the computer?' her nephew asked.

'The computer is in my bedroom,' she answered sternly. 'And it's off-limits. I use it only for business.'

She thought she caught the trace of a smile

about Parker's lips as he seemed to struggle to remain serious and uninvolved with the discussion.

She finished her business with Roger. 'The phone is on the kitchen counter. Pick it up and dial one-one-three if you want to reach the front desk by my office. Got that?'

'Yeah,' said Roger. 'One-one-three.'

Parker busied himself looking out the French doors in this room at the view over the apple tree grove to the east.

'No mountain view,' she said, noticing Parker looking out as well. 'I'm on the east side.'

'Nice, though,' he said.

'Well, thanks again,' said Jenny. 'We've kept you long enough.'

She needed to get back to work herself.

'Roger, why don't you unpack? You can use that dresser and this closet. Do you have homework to do?'

For answer he shrugged, but he snapped open one of the suitcases.

'You can study on the dining room table if you like.'

'What time is dinner?'

She sighed. 'I'm afraid I don't have any groceries yet. I meant to shop after work. I didn't know you'd be coming, so we'll have to eat in the facility dining room tonight.

Dinner's in an hour. I'll come and get you. Will you be all right here until then?'

'Sure,' he said. 'No problem.'

Now why didn't she like the conniving gleam in his beady brown eyes? She would have to remember all she knew about her nephew, so she could stay one step ahead of him. But she didn't have time to think about that right now.

She and Parker returned to the living room, where he admired some gold-framed photographs on her mantel. A twinge in her heart admitted curiosity for a man who had been laid off, mutual parting of the ways or not. And she wondered if he'd had to sell a house. Well, that was none of her business. Let Grace Douglas ferret out all those personal details if she were so inclined.

'Those are my parents,' she explained. 'And that's my sister, Maureen. She's Roger's mother. You barely missed meeting her.'

'Nice family.'

'Yes.'

Another twinge. Did he have family other than his mother? She couldn't remember anything about Dorothy McAllister's situation at the moment.

His brown eyes found hers and he held her gaze pleasantly, but he didn't say anything. She stammered to continue the conversation.

'Do you have other relatives — besides your mother, I mean?'

Why was she asking him something so personal? All she needed to do was be polite.

'I have a daughter. She's eight.'

'Oh.' For some reason that surprised her.

There was a flash of pain in his deep brown eyes, and Jenny realized that she had never seen a man with such expressive eyes before. But the rest of his chiseled face remained impassive.

'What's her name?' she asked, before she could stop the words coming out of her mouth.

'Sydney.' He smiled, but there was a melancholy to it.

Uh oh, Jenny thought. She was treading on dangerous territory here, and it wasn't any of her business. But they could talk about his mother; that *was* her business.

She walked him to the door. In the back of her mind, she worried about leaving Roger here alone. But surely he couldn't get into too much trouble in just an hour.

'See you later,' she called out to Roger.

Then she accompanied her other visitor into the hallway and locked the door behind her.

'Can I give you a lift back?' Parker asked as they waited for the elevator.

'I'd better walk,' she said, her hand fluttering to her chest. 'I haven't had much exercise today.'

Outside, they stood in the bright sun. A cold breeze from the west made itself felt, and they both glanced at the heavy layer of gray clouds headed their way from the mountains to the northwest.

'Guess we might get that snow,' he said, judging the weather.

As for other Denverites, the weather was a common subject. The high altitude and proximity to the mountains made for rapidly changing weather in this dry climate. Sunny and warm one day, a blizzard the next; you never knew what to expect. Neither did the meteorologists, half the time.

'Well, thanks for the tree,' she said again.

'Yeah, no problem.'

He didn't seem anxious to get into his truck. 'It's nice to meet you, Jenny Knight.'

'Just Jenny,' she said, a little nervous at the sound of her name on his lips. 'Will you be visiting your mother while you're here?'

'I'll drop in to say hi. But I can't stay long. This is a busy week for Christmas trees.'

'Oh, yes.'

'But I believe I have a little business with your program director.'

Jenny felt a ping of surprise. Had Grace

mobilized so fast in Parker's direction?

She stared at him. A hint of amusement crossing his face made her think he'd read her mind. But his explanation was simple.

'I sponsor my daughter's school choir. Miss Douglas has arranged for them to sing carols here tomorrow evening. I think you're having a tree-decorating party.'

'Oh, yes, of course. Then you and Grace will have things to discuss.'

Parker got into his truck to move it back to the parking area in front. Jenny decided she did need to walk through the complex. It would help her get her mind back on business, and help her think of what to do with Roger.

Once in the east wing of the building, she put on her professional smile and greeted the residents as she passed them in the halls, pausing to talk to some of them. Many of them had been here for ten years or more and had known her grandmother. How would they feel now if they knew they were in danger of losing their home? It made her clench her jaw with renewed determination that that would not happen.

If they survived the corporate office's inspection and managed to keep the doors open, she had plenty of ideas in mind that the elderly folks who lived here would benefit from. Most of them had interesting stories to tell. She wanted to make a project out of having them all interviewed about their histories. The stories would make an entertaining and memorable book they could print up for the residents and their families. But she hadn't even brought that up with Grace yet, because they didn't have the budget for printing such a project right now.

By the time she regained the main lobby and crossed to her office in the northwest corner of the building, she was once again enveloped in the affairs of the retirement home. Part of her mind tried to ignore the warm fuzziness she'd experienced in meeting Parker McAllister. The rest of her attention dwelled on the fact that two weeks with her nephew in a retirement home was a contradiction in terms.

2

Parker found his mother watering some plants on a rolling cart that sat before her sunny window. Every time he stepped into the warm, comfortable apartment located on the third floor of the retirement home, he absorbed the coziness of the place. He still felt some qualms that he hadn't moved his mother into his own home. But Dorothy McAllister had been adamant that selling her condo and moving here had been the best solution.

And he had to admit that, if she lived with him, she would have little opportunity to see her friends. Most of her friends and social contacts were in their mid- to late seventies themselves. Few of them drove anymore. And since Parker had left Millennium Electronics, he'd been working from dawn 'til nine o'clock at night at the Christmas tree lot. That left little time to entertain Mom.

Here at the Cherry Valley Retirement Home she was with people in her own age group, whom she saw at nearly every meal. And the intrepid Grace Douglas kept them busy all the time.

'Hi, Mom.' He closed the door behind him.

'Parker, dear, you're early. Did you bring the tree?'

He gave his mom a kiss on her cool cheek. He took the watering can from her and deposited it on the counter at the end of the living room next to the kitchen sink. A standing screen separated oven, sink and refrigerator from the living-dining area. A door to the left led to her small bedroom. And beyond that was a study. A nice arrangement as these things went. And with her furnishings from the condo, it looked like home.

'Yes, I did,' he replied to her question about the tree. 'It's standing downstairs now.'

'How did you get it in?'

'I had some help.'

He smiled to himself, thinking about the two women marshaling the placement of the tree and the skinny kid who'd helped. He didn't quite know the story behind the kid and the general manager, Jenny Knight, but it made him curious.

And he was even more aware of the chemistry between himself and Jenny. There was something about the way she'd walked and the inviting look of her lush, wavy auburn hair curling around her cheeks and the fine, generous brows over liquid, light-brown eyes

27

and long, slender nose. The way she carried her straight shoulders and kept her professional demeanor in place didn't cover up some inner vulnerability in those eyes. He judged her to be about thirty-two years old. And he knew she'd only been on this job for about three months. The tightness in her shoulders told him she was struggling to master the responsibility. And the shield of armor she'd erected all around herself said *keep away*. That was fine with him, since he wasn't looking for a woman right now.

But he'd read the doubtful expression in Jenny Knight's eyes when she'd directed her nephew to do his homework. She wasn't used to kids. A little like his ex, Sheila, that way. Women were so career-oriented nowadays. Few of them were nurturing in the old-fashioned way. Maybe he was old-fashioned, himself. Sheila had been career-oriented when they'd gotten married. Getting pregnant had been an accident, but one he'd never regretted, for it gave them Sydney, his joy in life. But Sheila had not been happy to be pregnant.

Parker's mind was wandering. He brought his attention back to his mother, dressed as attractively as usual in a lavender suit that complemented her white hair and bright blue eyes. She had taken a seat in the chocolate-colored stuffed armchair. He folded his long body onto the beige-striped sofa next to it.

'I can't stay long, Mom. I have a meeting with your program director, and then I've got to get back to the lot to make sure Gary's kids are keeping up with things.'

His mother's soft blue gaze reached out with a look of loving concern. 'Are you working too hard, son?'

'Mom, you know I don't want to start serious job hunting for another few months. When Gary had his heart attack and asked me to take over the lot, I looked at this as an opportunity to do something physical and be outdoors for a change. I'm taking time to think about what I want to do next.'

He reached over and laid his big hand on hers, giving it a squeeze.

'It was time for a change,' he told her.

His mother tried to smile, but she still looked worried. 'Being vice president in charge of marketing at that electronics company was a big responsibility,' she said. 'I know you did your best.'

'Yeah, and I was good at what I did. But after the merger, they couldn't keep us all. I looked at it as a chance to start over.'

That was the easiest way to explain to his mother that he hadn't felt at home in the super-corporate structure. Probably would have wound up with a heart attack himself if he'd stayed on. He'd gone against his free spirit long enough. He wanted to be happy.

She squeezed his hand, her blue eyes looking deep into his soul, the way she'd always been able to do. 'I know you took Gary's lot because of your kind heart. You always want to help people.'

'I don't know about that,' Parker said, shaking his head. 'I've never been completely sure I did the right thing by moving you in here. You have to promise to let me know if you don't like it here. You can always move out to the house.'

Dorothy grunted and waved that idea away.

'I know, son. Not all people my age are so lucky. And I would enjoy being with you and Sydney when you have her. But I don't believe in a mother being underfoot all the time. You need your own space.'

She looked at him more closely. 'How are the two of you getting along?'

Her look said she didn't mean to pry but was concerned for her son and granddaughter anyway. It also asked a silent question that he wasn't willing to answer. What about his love life? his mother's eyes asked. He knew his mother would be happy if he remarried. But she wouldn't want him to marry again until he found the right woman. And he didn't think the right woman walked the earth.

A picture of Jenny Knight flashed into his mind for some reason, but he dismissed it. Momentary attractions didn't mean anything.

When he'd been divorced, six years ago, Sheila had gotten custody of their now eight-year-old daughter. It had been rough at first. He never missed a child-support payment, but his heart had an empty spot from the years he'd missed quality time with his daughter. He was making up for some of that now, taking Sydney on weekends. He knew that Sheila wanted more freedom, and he didn't care what she did with her life unless it affected Sydney. He tried not to show his frustrations at what a mess his home life was.

'We're fine,' he said to his mother. 'I'll have Sydney tomorrow, before the Christmas caroling.'

He gave his mother an amused, wry look. 'I understand from Grace Douglas that you've been roped into some scriptwriting for the big Christmas program in two weeks.'

Dorothy McAllister managed to look impish. 'I volunteered for the committee. We're to write the program in coordination with the music and Grace's ideas about bringing in a few animals. A great pageant, it is to be.'

He didn't miss the mischievous light that shined in his mom's eyes.

'Grace wants to include Sydney's choir too,' he told her. 'As sponsor, I guess I'm involved.'

Dorothy nodded, a bemused, speculative look in her eyes. She tilted her head slightly.

'I think Grace wants us all to have dinner together tomorrow night before the tree-decorating. Will that be convenient for you and Sydney?'

'No problem. We'll be here anyway. We'll both need to clean up after work, and Sydney will need to change into her choir robe. Mind if we impose?'

'Of course not.'

Dorothy didn't hold his gaze, and he immediately became suspicious. Despite his insistence that he had no time to date, there was a bit of the matchmaker in his mother. Of course, she wanted to see her son happy. But he had to give her a warning look.

'Something tells me I should beware of my match-making mother.'

'Oh, no, nothing like that,' protested Dorothy. 'What you do is your business.'

He felt a surge of affection for her. She was just looking out for his own good in her own way.

Then her thin gray eyebrows wrinkled in concern. 'So, you have to work tomorrow.'

He still wished she wouldn't look at him

like that. In spite of his trying to convince her that he *liked* selling Christmas trees after the pressures of marketing electronics, she didn't seem to believe him. He wondered suddenly if he had disappointed her. After all, she and Dad had scraped together the money to get him a fine education and master's degree on top of it.

His dad had been a civil servant all his working years, working in the post office for the last ten years before his retirement. So his folks had had a comfortable retirement and solid health benefits. And Parker had been able to get started on his own career. Maybe after thirteen years of doggedly climbing the corporate ladder, his mother pitied his downfall. And that galled him. He didn't take well to pity.

'Gary's boys will work tomorrow afternoon. I'll be able to bring Sydney here later.'

Dorothy lifted a brow. 'I thought you said you had to pick her up in the early afternoon.'

'I do,' he admitted.

'Are you going to have her sit around with you at the lot until you're free?' A note of disapproval laced his mother's tone.

A sting of guilt suffused his reply as well. 'She can help out. She enjoys showing customers the trees.'

'Parker, really. There are child labor laws.'

'But a child likes to contribute. Truly.' He gave his mother his most boyish, charming smile. 'Sydney loves my new job. She knows it's the source of her support. It makes her feel able and competent to know she's helping me earn money.'

His mother looked a little skeptical but didn't say anything.

'Mom, I had a paper route when I was twelve. It's okay for kids to work.'

His mother pressed her lips together, not quite arguing with him. 'As long as she gets time to play with friends her own age. Children should play.'

Another sore point. Parker hadn't been able to get as much information out of Sheila about Sydney's playmates as he would like. Sydney was doing well at school, and she was spokesperson of the children's choir. But when it came to Sydney's friends, Sheila didn't reveal much. Another reason he wanted to spend more time with Sydney and find out what was on her mind. He realized guiltily how little he'd actually taken time to listen to his daughter in their usually activity-filled weekends. What did she think about? What were her concerns?

'What are you frowning about?' asked Dorothy.

'Oh, I was just thinking about new friends

for Sydney. Your general manager, Jenny Knight, has a nephew who just came to stay with her for a couple of weeks.'

'A nephew? How old is he?'

'Eleven or so,' mused Parker.

His mother chuckled. 'Parker dear, eleven-year-old boys are petrified by little girls, unless they are able to show off in front of them.'

He leaned down to peck at his mother's curly white head. 'You're probably right. Don't get up, Mom. I'll see you tomorrow.'

'Take care, dear.'

At the door, he turned to wave to her, counting his blessings. After all their mutual losses, they could still count on each other.

★ ★ ★

Jenny hunched over the printout of the December calendar spread on her big oak desk. Grace leaned forward from the chair opposite, pencil tapping out the dates. They were going over the December programs one last time before Grace had the calendar printed in the newsletter. Jenny frowned and moved her hands from supporting her chin up into her wavy auburn hair.

'Don't you think bringing live animals for this Christmas extravaganza is going a little far, Grace? We're not insured for damage from livestock.'

Grace waved an arm, her hand just missing the green-shaded brass lamp on the corner of the desk.

'Not a problem. The trainers will take care of them. They do programs like this in big churches all the time. People love live animals. It will be splendid.'

She slid an eleven-by-seventeen-inch sketch under Jenny's nose.

'Here's the layout. The risers for the children's choir will be here.'

The pencil eraser thumped and bounced on the sheet.

'The small stage for the stable will go in the center.' Another tap. 'And the trainer is bringing one of those portable pens for the sheep.'

Jenny placed a hand on her forehead. 'Sheep! Must we?'

She counted to ten and then said, 'There is no budget for cleaning up after these animals.'

'Not a problem,' said Grace. 'The trainers will take care of that. It's written into their agreements.'

Jenny had a fleeting thought of collecting the stuff for fertilizer, but she dismissed it as impractical.

'All right, if you are *sure* the trainers have signed contracts saying they are responsible for their animals. Do you have a list of the animals and trainers?'

'Right here — '

A knock interrupted them, and both women's heads jerked up to see Parker McAllister filling the open doorway. Jenny's heart bumped in surprise, and she sat up straighter. Men like that were always aware of how casually sexy they looked, leaning against a door jamb. This one probably practiced it a hundred times a day, just for effect.

'Can we help you?' she said, dropping the papers on her desk.

She glanced at Grace, who had twisted around to stare at Parker in open appreciation.

Jenny cleared her throat. 'Oh, I forgot. You two have a meeting.'

One side of his mouth lifted in good humor. 'Just a few words, really. I wanted to make sure the tree was satisfactory, and Miss Douglas wanted to confirm the time for my daughter's choir tomorrow evening.'

Grace twisted the rest of her body around on the gray upholstered chair.

'Call me Grace,' she said, rising to face him.

Jenny remained seated, feeling a little foolish.

But if Parker was disconcerted by Grace's open friendliness, he kept his suave manners.

'The carolers will get here by six. Will that work for you?'

'Excellent,' replied Grace. 'They can form up and sing to their little hearts' content for as long as they like.'

She explained to Jenny, 'The tree decorating party was already on the schedule for tomorrow night. When I ordered the tree, I thought it might be nice to have the kiddies' choir come along and sing as entertainment. When it became apparent that Mr. McAllister himself was the choir's sponsor, I couldn't resist making the request.'

Jenny tried a reassuring smile in Parker's direction. 'That is generous of you.'

He grinned back. His scrutinizing brown eyes found hers across the distance of the room, though he had now taken a couple of steps inside.

'Oh, I just get the rides organized, that's all, really.'

'I see,' said Jenny. 'Well, of course we appreciate it. We have room for the choir in the commons area across from the parlor. Will the group need risers?'

He shook his head. 'It's only twenty or so kids. They'll be fine in a couple of rows on the floor.'

From behind her desk, Jenny was having a hard time keeping her eyes off his appealing mouth and the warmth in his eyes. She had to acknowledge his attractiveness, but she reminded herself that she was not looking for a date, even if Grace so obviously was.

Jenny's emotions were raw from her having been dumped three months earlier by her jet-setting rake of a former boyfriend. In her heart of hearts, she would forever beware of men like Parker McAllister. And it would be unethical for her to become involved with the relative of any of the Cherry Valley residents. In her position as general manager of the place, she knew Parker McAllister was safely off-limits. And that was a good thing.

'Uh, oh, fine,' she said.

She drew in a deep breath, threw her shoulders back and looked professional.

'The party starts at six-thirty. Grace will take care of the details.'

'Of course, of course,' said Grace, circling her chair and leaning her hands against the back of it as if she were a general preparing for battle. 'A great inspiration occurred to me earlier, which I will now propose.'

Both Jenny and Parker turned to stare at her.

She gestured broadly, including both of them. 'We shall have a dinner meeting tomorrow evening before the party.'

Her green eyes and proud smile glowed with the self-acknowledged brilliance of her plan. She then elaborated.

'Our children's choir sponsor will already be here, and his daughter as representative of that choir. It so happens that Parker's mother, Dorothy, is my head scriptwriter. She can speak for her entire committee.'

She gave Jenny a conspiratorial glance, as if they were hatching a great strategy. 'And as our fearless leader you will be needed to listen to plans from all sides.'

Grace slapped the chair. 'This is the way to get everyone involved and get things done.'

Irrational confusion spiraled through Jenny. If Grace wanted to marshal the handsome Parker McAllister into a dinner meeting, that was one thing. She, herself, would rather avoid any further contact with the man. But she also needed to keep a tight rein on Grace and her expansive plans for the upcoming Christmas production.

Parker was still looking at her. Did she imagine it, or did his thick, dark lashes, droop just slightly over those dreamy eyes? *Oh, stop it*, she told herself. Let Grace daydream about those gorgeous eyes. Jenny just wasn't going to get roped in by good looks again. She'd learned her lesson once and for all, the hard way: Never trust a handsome, desirable man, especially the kind that make your insides quiver.

'Very well,' she said to Grace reluctantly. She didn't see a way to refuse. 'If you think we need to discuss it over dinner, I suppose it's a good idea.'

She tilted her swivel chair back a couple of inches, her arms gripping the armrests. She gave Grace a warning look, then smoothed her features to glance at Parker.

'Is there anything else I can do for you?'

One of his dark eyebrows cocked upward. 'I did want to talk to you about one of my mother's concerns. But that can wait.'

She eased her chair down and reached for her appointment book. If Dorothy had a concern, she'd better hear about it.

'I'm always happy to listen to any of the residents' concerns. Would you like to set up an appointment?

She flipped a page, realizing her hand was trembling unprofessionally. She looked up at him again.

'I'm, uh, free tomorrow before the party, but of course you'll be busy transporting the kids then.'

He leaned his head to the side, his sensual lips serious.

'That is a possibility. The other parents are

bringing the kids. Maybe I could take a few minutes of your time before the . . . ' He paused, glancing at Grace. 'The dinner meeting,' he continued. 'Mom won't mind watching Sydney for half an hour or so.'

Then Jenny slumped. 'Oh, dear, I forgot about Roger.'

Drat. How *was* she going to carry out her weekend responsibilities with her nephew underfoot? He was old enough to take care of himself most of the time, but she couldn't ignore him completely. She just knew that would be taking too much of a chance. And what had her sister said about the tuba lesson? She scratched her head, trying to remember.

Parker seemed aware of her thought process. His handsome face looked sympathetic.

'Maybe Roger would like to meet my daughter.'

Jenny stared at him as if he'd come from another planet. Introduce Roger to a girl? She was nonplussed.

Parker gave a deep chuckle that affected her insides.

'I know boys that age,' he said. 'Girls are not their favorite playmates. But it might be good for both of them to practice being polite to each other. And Roger might be able to contribute some ideas for the program. Give him something creative to do.'

She saw then the flicker of something like tenderness in his eyes. Some well-hidden concern for something. But she didn't know him or his situation well enough to judge just what he was reaching for. Did his daughter need to make some friends?

She leaned back thoughtfully. Grace was still in the room, leaning forward expectantly, but Jenny felt a warm connection between herself and Parker that was awkwardly disconcerting. It was probably just that he was being so polite that it flattered her ego. But maybe this idea about getting the kids together wasn't a bad one. Roger could use some social graces. Why not give him the opportunity to practice them?

Her own smile emanated from the inside. *Bless you, Parker McAllister,* she thought silently. His notions about kids gave her some great ideas. She just might offer her nephew plenty of opportunity to contribute to life at the retirement home. After all, elderly people did enjoy seeing youngsters, as long as they remained well-behaved. She was still smiling when she got up to go around her desk and shake his hand. For a moment they just grinned foolishly at each other. It was then that she heard Grace cough.

'Oh,' said Jenny, stepping back and

dropping the strong, firm hand almost reluctantly. 'Well then, that's settled. We can meet at four-thirty. I'll have Roger join us in the lobby after that for dinner.'

'That'll be fine.'

He turned and strode back to the door. Then, with a slight wave, he bowed his head in acknowledgment to both ladies and disappeared around the corner.

'Now, that is a man,' said Grace, her hawkish eyes sending sparks of interest.

Jenny's lips tightened as she thought about the discipline that was necessary in this situation.

'Grace, I hope you're not harboring any ideas about Parker McAllister.'

The aggressive program director blinked. 'Who wouldn't harbor ideas about such a one? A rare catch, if I do say so myself.'

She batted her eyelashes, which looked ridiculous on her squarish face.

Jenny didn't want to burst Grace's bubble, but she couldn't hold her tongue either. It wasn't exactly against the rules for her staff to flirt with relatives of residents; it was only unspoken ethics that ought to prevent it. In her position of responsibility as leader of the community, it was the sort of thing she should be aware of.

'I'll admit he's good-looking,' Jenny said. 'He's also the son of one of our residents.'

'Not off-limits, is he?'

'Well, the corporate office might consider it unethical for me to get involved with a resident's family member. Not that I'm interested, of course.'

Grace clicked her tongue, as if she didn't quite agree. But that was the appealing thing about Grace Douglas; everything was out in the open and aboveboard.

Grace gave Jenny an examining look that seemed to delve deep. Jenny was the boss, but she could see Grace's thoughts churning away inside that plotting head of hers. Perhaps she wondered if Jenny had some more personal motives for mentioning it.

She began to feel annoyed with all these details, and recognized her own grumpiness on the subject of the holidays in general. Well, she couldn't dwell on any of this now; she had other meetings lined up. She initialed the papers they'd been going over before being interrupted by Parker and handed them back to Grace.

'You can get this printed. We'll talk more about the scope of the Christmas program tomorrow at your dinner. For now, I've approved the time and date.'

Grace gave her a look of honest assessment. Jenny tried to ease her face into a less rigid expression.

'I'm sorry if I sound abrupt,' she admitted. 'This is just a busy time. And you know everything has to be perfect when the corporate office descends on us in two weeks.'

'Indeed, that is true,' agreed Grace. 'There is a lot to be done.'

Grace packed the papers into a manilla folder and shoved it under her arm, sticking her pencil behind her ear.

'And speaking of that, I'd better go see about those Christmas tree decorations.'

The program director marched off to other pressing duties.

By the time Jenny had met with the kitchen supervisor to discuss new staff, gone over costs for the new sprinkler system being installed in all the units and read the statistics on move ins and move outs for the next few months, she felt fatigued. But no long, relaxing evening stretched ahead of her. It was time to go fetch Roger for supper in the common dining room.

Grace leaned into Jenny's office on her way out for the day.

'I'm leaving,' she said with a wave that looked something like a salute.

'Lucky you,' said Jenny before she realized the words were out of her mouth. Then she added, 'Sorry. I'm just a little tired.'

Grace shook her head in sympathy. 'And you having to baby-sit. What luck.'

'Yeah. But it can't be too bad.'

'Well,' said Grace, on a rising tone, 'I'll be here by three o'clock sharp tomorrow, to get things organized. Got to be ready for the assault on that tree.'

'Thanks, Grace.' Jenny rocked back in her swivel chair and tried to marshal a smile. 'Couldn't do it without you.'

Then Jenny got up and followed Grace out into the lobby, suddenly wishing she, too, were going farther away than just to the next building. She watched as the ever-cheerful, ever-friendly Grace stopped to chat with some of the elderly residents on her way out the front doors. Jenny stifled a wave of envy. How could Grace always be so happy? Didn't she ever feel the weight of life and work around her shoulders? What was she so happy about, anyway?

Jenny plastered a smile on her face to walk through the building. She wondered suddenly if she'd been wrong to take this job. She'd accepted the offer as a subtle way of proving to people like Drake that she could do a job that required her to give a lot of herself. And saving her late grandmother's last place of residence was just such a mission. But now that she was faced with this demanding

47

situation every day, she secretly wondered if she were up to it.

She wasn't selfless. She'd been rather spoiled as an adolescent, and old habits were hard to break. She used to indulge in lots of time for herself, thinking that if she pleased herself first, she would be better able to please others as well. But three months ago that had all turned upside down. Drake had followed a blond sales rep home from the sporting goods store one day and evidently decided that sport with her was preferable to his commitment to Jenny. At least he'd had the decency to call and tell her it was over.

She remembered her conversation with her mother shortly after that as if it had been yesterday.

'We always tried to make you the center of our lives, dear,' her mother had said in a rare heart-to-heart talk.

Jenny had gone to visit her parents in Seattle to try to get over feeling sorry for herself.

'I just hope I didn't do wrong as a mother. We always wanted you to have everything you wanted. Dad was the same way. Nothing was too good for his darling daughter.'

'I know, Mom, and I appreciate it,' Jenny had said.

They'd been sitting at her parents' kitchen

counter, overlooking a finger of water lushly bordered with trees. Her mother had looked at her with concern.

'What I mean is, dear, that I hope we didn't spoil you too much.'

Spoiled; there it was again. 'I know I'm used to having things my own way.' She had pulled a regretful expression. 'Drake thinks I don't care about anyone but myself.'

'I know that's not true,' said Mrs. Knight. 'He's just trying to defend himself.'

'Well, whichever of us is selfish, it obviously wasn't love, was it? If it's love, you don't worry about the other person being selfish, do you?'

'No dear, you don't.' Mrs. Knight sighed. 'Your father and I only wanted to give each other the very best. I just hope you'll find a man you feel that way about someday, dear.'

'Mmmm.'

Jenny had pondered that conversation all the way back to Denver. What did it mean to want to give everything to someone else? Surely when that happened, the other person would want to give everything back to you too. Well, it certainly hadn't been the time for that.

With her MBA, she had qualified for the job here at Cherry Valley. She needed to do something noble. Working in a retirement home was not a job for a selfish person, the owners of the company had told her. And since her little talk with her mother, Jenny had decided it was time to prove to herself and to other people that she was capable of saving something.

'I am a very hard worker,' she had told the female Human Resources director of Cherry Valley Retirement Homes, International. 'And I do get along with older people.'

'You may find your patience tried at times,' the impeccably dressed HR director had told her. 'It's not going to be easy to turn the establishment around financially while at the same time trying to make sure you and your staff don't ignore the needs of the residents. It's a fine line you'll be walking.'

'I'm sure I can do it,' Jenny had assured her after they went over her credentials.

Maybe it was just stubborn, spoiled pride that wanted to prove them all wrong, she wondered now. *I, Jenny Knight, do not have to be selfish. I do not. I care about the place Grandma loved, and for her sake and her friends, I will not allow it to close its doors.*

She pushed open the door to her apartment to the loud blare of music coming from her stereo. The noise set her teeth on edge, and she marched over to turn the volume down.

'Roger,' she called.

He slouched out of the bedroom, adjusting his glasses, as if she, and not he, were a specimen inside an aquarium. She took a deep breath, determined to be civilized.

'Please don't play the stereo so loud. In an apartment like this, you have to consider the neighbors. These walls are thin. Besides, the reggae version of 'I Want to Wish You a Merry Christmas' is not meant to be played so loud.'

Roger peered up through his glasses. 'Why not?'

She shut her eyes once and opened them. 'Reggae is a soft, easy rhythm. It's not alternative rock.'

'I couldn't find any Barenaked Ladies in your CDs.'

'That's because I don't have any. I enjoy soft,' she almost said *romantic*, 'uh, relaxing music.'

He shrugged and strolled over to the refrigerator to open the door. She followed and shut it.

'We're eating in the dining room tonight, remember? Are you ready?'

''Course. What're we having?'

'Probably pasta. But you can order a sandwich, if you prefer.'

'Can I have both?'

'Yes, you can have both if you can eat both. But I don't want food to be wasted.'

And at the end of his visit, she would send her sister a bill for all the food he ate while he was here.

3

Saturday morning was brisk and cold, the way a fine December day should be. After weeks of unseasonable warmth, the cold snap was good for business at the Christmas tree lot. Parker loaded a fifteen-foot Douglas fir into the back of a minivan and then brushed himself off to accept the woman's payment.

The expensively dressed, artfully made-up blond woman gave him a quick once-over as she handed him the bills.

'Are those your sons?' she asked, glancing past him at the two teenage boys helping other customers.

Parker recognized the lowered eyelids for what they implied. She was interested. But he wasn't. In his most pleasant manner, he turned her come-on around with his next words.

'No. They're my employees. I took over this business from a sick friend.'

'Oh.'

She pursed outlined, mauve lips and put the change in her expensive wallet, which she tucked into her suede purse. Her penciled eyebrow lifted.

'How's business?'

'Excellent,' he replied. 'Especially on these cold days. Things were a little slow during all the sunny days we had last week.'

He shook his head, clucking his tongue. 'I had a friend who sold trees in New York one winter. Lost everything in the last two weeks before Christmas because of the weather. Too warm,' he said seriously.

He finished tying the doors of her minivan together. The tree was too long to allow them to close, but he secured everything, then stepped back and brushed his gloved hands together.

'You should be fine to drive home now.'

He stood back, hands folded over his money belt. She gave him a look of regret, and he shook his head as she stepped away. He was learning a lot about what people thought of you just by what you did for a living. One more comeuppance he was getting used to in his present, humble position. Or, should he say, in the real world.

The woman got into the van and put on her sunglasses. The morning was cold, but Denver's sun was bright, even in winter. The well-heeled society woman had decided that a man who sold Christmas trees for a living off a temporary outdoor lot wasn't worth pursuing. Not that he would have taken her up on it. He wasn't into that sort of thing anymore.

Working outdoors on these crisp mornings were the best time for thinking. The cold, dry air seemed to clear his mind. Parker McAllister, promising young business tycoon turned Christmas tree expert, surveyed his kingdom, a half-acre lot located in Denver's upscale Cherry Creek area. The lot was leased from a developer who hadn't yet started construction on another row of expensive town houses. A small trailer had come with the lot, where Parker had set up a temporary office for the business.

He headed back up the slope to where Gary's teenage kids, Preston and Frankie, were handling a couple of other customers. It was early in the day yet. The rush would probably come later. Parker stretched his legs and strode on up to the top of the lot, where he could examine the rows of trees. Douglas firs, Fraser firs and blue spruce from the tree farm in Black Forest. Trees from three to sixteen feet. Bigger trees were special-ordered.

Satisfaction swelled inside him. Such a simple life, but he was enjoying it even more than he might have expected. Severance pay would keep him afloat until he found a real job. But he had not been anxious to have the executive search firm send him out on interviews yet. God, how he had pushed himself the last thirteen years. Even before that, in college and graduate school, his parents had pushed him for the best grades. Then, when he'd fallen for Sheila's good looks and social status, he'd pushed himself even harder. Sheila had been a woman who'd wanted a lot. And as a young man with raging hormones, he'd been twisted around her little finger.

Of course, they had been blessed with Sydney. The thought of his eight-year-old daughter brought a stab of regret for the divorce Sydney had had to watch her parents go through. But the sting was mellowed by the grin on his chilly lips. Because of his present job, he'd been able to see more of her. And she loved the Christmas trees. He consulted his watch, unconsciously calculating the number of hours until he could take a break and pick her up. It would be warmer this afternoon too, so that if Sydney wanted to help them out here, she wouldn't get too chilled.

A tan Mercedes swerved into the lot and stopped. Behind the wheel he saw another pair of designer sunglasses on an undoubtedly well-made-up face. The lot was located near some of the most expensive Denver real estate. Town homes and condos for blocks needed his fine trees to fill their double-paned windows. And they were willing to pay his prices.

It also meant being dealt some new attitudes. Attitudes he'd never even dreamed of when he'd been vice president of marketing at Millennium Electronics. In his corner office in the Denver Tech Center, the only time he ever met a street vendor was when he stopped to buy a hot dog, when he didn't have to go to a business lunch.

He realized now that the longest exchange he'd ever had with the hot-dog seller had been comments about the weather. Where did the man live? Did he come far to sell to the Tech Center crowd? Funny how things looked now that he was a small vendor himself, bowing and scraping to the wealthy clients who shopped in upscale Cherry Creek. If there was anything that Parker had learned from parting company with the corporate world, it was that what he'd been brought up to believe was a classless society was far from it.

Of course the women who came to buy his trees recognized the fact that he had blood in his veins. Some of them looked at his fit body and speculated about the pumping of that blood. But as soon as he demonstrated that he wasn't doing this as a hobby, Cherry Creek's wealthy single women gave him the cold shoulder.

Parker McAllister, thirty-seven-year-old free spirit and philosopher, broke off his musings and walked down the slope to wait on some more customers.

Just as he predicted, business picked up later. The day remained cold at thirty degrees, but he hardly noticed it in his long underwear, flannel shirt and winter parka. At eleven o'clock, he checked with red-haired seventeen-year-old Frankie and his dark-haired older brother, Preston, who assured him that they could handle things while he went to pick up Sydney.

The little light of his life lived with her mother in an elegant sandstone brick home Parker referred to as the castle. A round, beige brick turret next to a bay window gave it the look. And the tall, sloped lot gave the impression of the medieval mound on which the first English castles were built.

He and Sheila were civil to each other, and Parker even had a passing acquaintance with her new husband, Melville. He, of course, was everything Parker wasn't any longer — a lawyer with an old, established firm. Melville and Sheila belonged to the Denver Country Club. And since she didn't have to work,

Sheila kept busy with charity organizations, making sure to get her picture in the society pages of the Sunday paper as often as possible.

'Daddy!' came a high-pitched scream, as the front door banged open and eight-year-old Sydney flew out to the porch and down the front steps.

'Hey,' he called, opening his arms for her to fly into them for a hug. He whirled her around on the grass before setting her down, his own joyous chuckles mingling with her bubbling laughter.

'Ready to go, chicken?'

'I'm not a chicken.'

The rosy-cheeked eight-year-old put her hands on her hips and screwed up her face at him. He tousled her brown hair, done in two ponytails. Tangled bangs fell across her forehead above expressive turquoise eyes. Sydney's eyes weren't just plain blue; they were a brilliant aquamarine and looked as if they'd come from the sea.

But then, Parker was given to waxing eloquent over his daughter. Looking at her in her Norwegian-patterned sweater and blue corduroy pants, his chest swelled with the love he felt. And then there was the slice of knowledge that cut through the back of his mind every time he saw her. He could love his daughter perfectly. Too bad he'd never found a mate with whom he could share such feelings.

The front door opened again and he shaded his eyes against the sun to see his ex-wife poke her head out. Her shiny brunette hair was darker than Sydney's, and while Sydney had her mother's fine-boned face, the eight-year-old had none of the imperiousness that Sheila carried about her perfectly clothed body.

'Hi,' he said to his ex.

'Parker, I'm so glad you're here. I've got to run off to my opera guild meeting. I've got Sydney's things packed. Her choir robe and bow are in a garment bag.'

He strode up to the porch and stepped inside the hardwood-floored foyer to lean down and pick up the luggage for Sydney's weekend. Then he listened to Sheila's ream of instructions about what their daughter should and should not do. As if he couldn't ask Sydney herself if she had any homework and to tell him when she was hungry.

He nodded to the impeccably made-up face as if he was listening, wondering for the hundredth time what had ever attracted him to her in the first place. There had been no romantic lust between them for years. Her trim body reminded him more of a perfect mannequin than of a human being who was a mother. When had she lost her warmth? When had they lost what had once been between them? Certainly it must have been years before the divorce. How much of it had been his fault?

'Don't worry,' he mumbled to her absently. 'We'll be fine.'

Sheila followed him out and bent down for Sydney to place a kiss on her smooth cheek. Then she stood to watch them get into the pickup truck. Her blue eyes flashed disapproval at the sight of her daughter climbing into the utilitarian vehicle.

'Why aren't you driving the Volvo?'

'Can't haul trees in it,' he said with a grin before he shut his door.

Sydney was all smiles — beaming, in fact, in the high front seat, where she could see over the smaller cars around them.

'Now, how about my girl coming with me to the Christmas tree lot?'

'Yes, yes,' she squealed.

Her wide smile showed perfect white teeth.

'All right, chicken. Buckle up.'

As they zoomed east on Sixth Avenue, he gave a warm chuckle, sending up a private prayer of thanks for this day that he could spend with his laughing, bouncing daughter.

The hours sped by with Sydney at the lot.

When she wasn't proudly naming the different kinds of trees for customers, Frankie and Preston tossed a football with her between the rows. She kept warm with hot chocolate from Parker's thermos and breaks inside the trailer. At three-thirty, he counted the take for the day so far and made out a slip for the night deposit slot at the bank.

Sydney's cheeks were red from the brisk winter day, and her hair had pulled partially out of the ponytails under her white cap, but her eyes were bright. When she climbed into the truck, she waved her mittened hands at the two young men who were taking over until nine o'clock tonight, when Parker would come back to secure the trees.

'You ready to get something to eat with Grandma?' he asked her, zipping up the money bag and stuffing it behind his seat.

She nodded vigorously. 'Mmmmmm. I could eat a horse.'

He grinned down at her. 'Well now, I don't know if they serve horses where we're going, but we'll ask for one.'

She waggled her head and laughed, and they shared the joke as he headed for the bank.

A half-hour later, Parker led Sydney through the front door of the Cherry Valley Retirement Home. As his eyes scanned the lobby, he found himself looking for the general manager. Out of the corner of his eye he spotted Grace Douglas, instead. She came forward to greet them.

Parker made introductions and Grace chatted with Sydney about singing in the children's choir tonight. But Parker's attention wasn't on them. As soon as he'd walked into the place, he knew he wanted to see Jenny Knight again. Not that it was a wise idea. She'd been almost rude to him, made it apparent that theirs was strictly a business relationship. It had almost seemed like they'd acknowledged the sparking attraction between them, and then had drawn the line. Obviously she wasn't looking for a man. Neither was he looking for a woman. With his future undecided, it wasn't the right time, and Sydney had to come first.

Something tugged at the corner of his mouth, thinking about that. Jenny Knight had made her displeasure apparent the first moment they'd met. It was he who had stared at her inviting body inside the very formal business suit, the skirt just short enough for him to imagine there was something feminine underneath all that armor. She had paid no attention to what he did for a living one way or the other. In fact, she'd done nothing to encourage him at all.

'The room is set up over here,' Grace was saying, directing them through the lobby toward the commons room.

Parker followed his daughter and the program director across the carpeted lobby to a large room with a hardwood floor and a grand piano. Chairs had been set up in a semicircle to one side.

Then he saw her.

Jenny was dressed in stirrup pants that emphasized her long, shapely legs, and a red, green and white sweater in a holiday pattern. Santas carried wreaths across her lovely breasts, and a piece of plastic holly had been jammed into her beautiful auburn hair, now twisted into a French braid. Damn! She was lovely. Parker felt a physical twinge at the sight of her. He could almost taste his attraction to her.

Being disgusted with the attitudes of the women he'd come across recently had only made him glad of his decision not to date. Since the divorce six years ago, there had been the occasional fling after parties given by his old cronies. But it was funny how he hadn't been invited to hang around with that crowd once he'd left his job.

The sudden surge of desire he experienced now caused Parker a bit of an inconvenience. He turned away from the sight of Jenny reaching upward to hang a decoration where one of the elderly residents pointed. Seeing her stretch like that was just too tempting a picture. Instead, he tried to focus on the room where the kids would sing.

Both Grace and Sydney were looking at him expectantly, and he realized that he must have missed something they said.

'Sorry,' he said, clearing his throat. 'I was looking at the tree over there. What were you saying?'

Grace's eyes flicked over to the tree and then back at him. He felt embarrassed that she seemed to read his mind. Still, he found Grace's open appraisal and her slightly lifted brow amusing. There was something about Grace that reminded him of his late sister, Anna, and Grace's almost masculine, direct approach was charmingly humorous.

He couldn't help but like her warm, earthy personality, though the camaraderie she inspired in him had nothing to do with the lust he was feeling for her boss. She seemed to know he'd been staring at Jenny, and he felt awkward.

'Our young choristers can change in the rest rooms on the other side of the lobby,' Grace said, taking charge again. 'But since Sydney's grandma lives here, I presume she will dress in Dorothy's abode?'

'Uh, right,' Parker said. 'We're headed that way now. Then we'll bring Mom down to the dining room for the, uh, dinner meeting. If we're still on for it.'

'Most certainly,' said Grace. 'Have to make sure we're all moving forward to the same tune, now, mustn't we?'

Grace leaned down to speak to Sydney again. 'I'll see you in a little while, then, Sydney. After your father's meeting with our general manager, we'll eat together and discuss plans for the big Christmas production. You can tell us what the choir is planning to sing two weeks hence.'

Sydney nodded her head. 'I know what we're singing.'

'Good, then.'

Parker smiled affably. Grace suddenly surprised him with a deliberate wink of one green eye. He just blinked, stunned, his mouth slightly open.

He didn't know quite how to deal with her rambunctious enthusiasm. As he took Sydney's hand and turned away, he could feel the program director's speculation grilling into the small of his back. It would have made him chuckle, if it hadn't made him confused.

★ ★ ★

Jenny had become aware of Parker McAllister in the big open commons room before she saw him. A movement of red flannel shirt and the sound of his voice came to her through the quiet conversations of the residents seated in the upholstered chairs grouped around the tree. Few of them were actually decorating, but from the happy smiles on their wrinkled faces, she could tell they were enjoying the proceedings. As she stretched for a branch above her head, she felt Parker's stare and turned to see him.

He looked at her approvingly for a moment, then was distracted from whatever thoughts were going around in that dark, handsome head of his by the little girl at his side. Jenny watched Grace bend down, hands braced on her locked knees, balancing herself. A garment bag was draped over Parker's arm.

Jenny's glance flew from the little girl with mussed ponytails to her father. She quickly assessed the similarities in facial features, but presumed that the daughter must have more of her mother in her physical makeup. She paused for a moment, hiding behind a branch, watching them speculatively. From a distance, she didn't see any harm in watching them. What had caused the divorce? she wondered. Financial strain? No, Grace had said his layoff had been recent, that the divorce had been prior to that. But it concerned her that he didn't have a secure job when he had a daughter to support. Though it really wasn't any of her business.

'I'm afraid that's all I can do right now,' she told the residents watching her. 'I have a brief meeting in my office before dinner. Will you all be here after dinner? The children's choir is going to sing carols for us.'

'Oh, sure, sure,' said the plump Mrs. McCallahan, an energetic elderly woman who'd been helping her. 'Wouldn't miss that.'

Jenny waved to the others, speaking to as many of them by name as she could. She was beginning to remember them all now.

Parker turned when Jenny crossed the room. She walked into his path as he and Sydney headed for the corridor leading to the apartments.

'Mr. McAllister,' she said in her professional voice. 'I haven't forgotten our meeting at four-thirty.'

His eyes grazed her, causing her heart to do a little dance in her chest.

'Nor have I.'

Now, why on earth did the look he gave her seem to make the earth move under her feet? This chemistry between them was becoming unnerving. But his gleaming eyes seemed to change from open appreciation to an inward determination to keep their relationship on a professional footing.

He, too, must certainly realize that it wasn't appropriate to flirt with the person who ran the establishment in which his mother lived. She disciplined herself to take only one long look at his chest covered by the flannel shirt. She noticed that his jeans had some traces of mud on them, and that his hair wasn't combed. But he gave her a disarming smile.

'We were just headed to my mother's to change.'

Ah, that explained it. He'd come straight from work. 'This must be Sydney,' she said.

He introduced her. 'Sydney, this is Miss Knight. She runs the place.'

Sydney stuck out her hand and Jenny was charmed at once. The round turquoise eyes examined her in a very adult fashion. She bent and shook Sydney's hand.

'I'm pleased to meet you, Sydney. We'll all be eating dinner together tonight. I hope you don't mind that my eleven-year-old nephew will be joining us for the meeting. He's staying with me for two weeks.'

Sydney rubbed her tummy and frowned expressively. 'I'm hungry. I was pretty busy at the Christmas tree lot. I don't care who eats with us.'

'That's good. Busy, were you?' said Jenny.

'Yes,' said Sydney with a bright smile. 'But I caught the football. Frankie and Preston showed me how.'

Jenny grinned. She would trade places with Parker in a minute. Having this perfectly well-behaved child stay with him all weekend would be much preferable to the unpredictable, moody eleven-year-old boy who was probably burning down her kitchen right now.

Her smile lingered as she shifted her gaze to Parker's. 'Then I'll see you in the lobby in about fifteen minutes?'

He nodded and glanced at Sydney. 'Come on, honey. Let's go to Grandma's and get ourselves cleaned up.'

Just at that moment a loud clattering ricocheted off the walls of the corridor leading to the first-floor apartments. Jenny recognized the sound of one of the utility carts being wheeled toward them much faster than was usual. On top of the cart was a large black case. As the cart trundled forward, she saw that Roger propelled it. Blindly.

'Oh, my God,' she groaned.

He reached the parlor area just as Mrs. O'Shay and Mr. Saito were pushing their walkers across to the commons room.

'Roger,' Jenny shouted, dashing toward the

cart to intercept it before the walkers and their owners became casualties. 'Slow down!'

Roger's head jutted around the case and the cart. Only then did he see the pedestrians in his path and jerk to a halt. But the big black case, with the weight of the tuba inside it, slid forward.

Jenny and Parker lunged at the same instant, and Parker caught the case as it threatened to fall off the edge of the cart. Jenny leaned on the cart, grasping her end for dear life. Her eyes flew to Parker's in grateful thanks as he eased the case back onto the cart.

'I'm sorry,' she said to all the surprised residents. 'Everyone all right?'

The voices of the residents rose at the excitement, and aides came flying from several directions. But the folks with the walkers and oxygen tanks were only startled, nothing more.

She turned around and hissed at Roger, 'Where did you get this cart?'

He shrugged. 'In the hallway. I was lugging the tuba here. When I got inside on the other end I saw the cart.'

She knew the door he referred to was the groundfloor entrance to assisted living. The nurse's aides used these carts to dispense medication. It was doubtful that an empty cart would be just sitting unused in the hall.

'Was there anything on the cart?' she interrogated her nephew.

He made a face. 'Just a couple of plastic cups. I figured it was trash, so I left them in the hall.'

'Roger! That was probably medication. A nurse's aide was probably very shocked when she came out into the hallway and found her medicine containers on the floor and the cart missing. Next time, ask someone first. All right?'

'Okay,' he said. But somehow she doubted the sincerity in his voice.

'Anyway, I got the tuba here, didn't I?' he challenged.

'Why do you need it here?'

He gave her that look of his, as if she were from another planet. 'Because I'm playing in the program tonight.'

She blinked, nonplussed. When had this been arranged?

'You are?'

He pointed a long finger toward Grace, who was fluttering between the residents and a maintenance man who was pushing the grand piano around the hardwood floor in the commons room.

'Mrs. Douglas said the children's choir was going to sing Christmas carols and they might need some accompaniment.'

She turned an accusing look at Grace, who had stopped at the sound of her name. A guilty expression spread across her features.

'Is that right?' Jenny asked Grace, who came toward them.

'Uh, well, he offered, and I didn't think I should refuse.' She played with the strand of colored beads lying on her green blouse.

Jenny sighed. 'Well, all right then.'

She pointed to the commons room.

'The program is in there,' she told Roger. 'I have a half-hour meeting with Mr. McAllister. Then you and I will eat dinner with some of the people involved in our Christmas production, including Mr. McAllister's daughter. Say hello to Sydney McAllister.'

Roger put his hands on his skinny hips and looked Sydney up and down. 'Hello.'

'Hello.'

'I'm eleven,' said Roger, hands still on his hips.

Sydney came forward from between her father's sheltering legs and stuck out her hand to Roger. 'I'm eight. I'm in second grade.'

They shook, Sydney pumping his thin hand, which Roger snatched back as soon as he could. Then he clamped his hand under his arm.

Jenny's eyes widened, and she hastened to intervene.

'Will you be ready to eat in half an hour?' she asked her nephew.

Roger went back to unzipping his tuba case. He frowned up at Jenny. 'Yeah.'

Parker and Jenny exchanged looks. Then Parker took his daughter's hand.

'We'd better get changed. I'll see you in about fifteen minutes,' he said to Jenny.

His glance shimmered across her, and then he turned to lead Sydney down the hall. Grace watched too, her own hands on her hips, a pleasant, almost dreamy expression on her squarish face. Jenny grunted at the absurdity of the situation, but she straightened her shoulders to confront Roger again.

'I know you're a lot older than Sydney,' said Jenny, 'but maybe you and she will find something in common to talk about.'

He grimaced. 'I don't have anything in common with girls.'

'Yes, you do,' said Jenny.

A small giggle tickled her throat. She felt suddenly clever, unused to such merriment.

'You're just about to play a Christmas program with a choir that is undoubtedly made up of over half girls. Did you think about that?'

74

He gave her a look that said she could walk over hot coals.

'I gotta warm up now.'

He surveyed the room in which the program would take place. 'Gotta check out the acoustics.'

Grace raised a generous brown eyebrow, and Jenny could not resist her own amusement. She didn't know they taught acoustics in sixth grade.

'Stay in here, then, until I come and get you,' she told Roger. 'And I don't think you'll want to leave your instrument unguarded while we eat. You can put it in that closet.'

'It's insured.'

Jenny shook her head at Grace and turned to seek refuge in her office.

Parker arrived there right on time for their scheduled appointment. She was waiting for him seated at her desk. When she looked up, she swallowed in consternation at how good he looked.

He had showered and changed into dark slacks and a red plaid oxford cloth shirt. A clean white T-shirt peeked out at the neck. His damp hair was combed back off his handsome forehead. Jenny was again conscious of the perfect symmetry of his face; rugged, yet almost glamorous with those thick, dark lashes. Altogether his looks made

Jenny's stomach do a somersault in spite of the talking-to she'd given herself about the matter.

She tried not to appear in the least interested as she motioned him in.

He took a step into the room, and then glanced over his shoulder. More than the usual hubbub drifted from the lobby down the short corridor to her office.

'Mind if I close the door?' he asked.

Her heart jumped into her throat.

'Uh, fine. I guess it is a little noisy out there.'

He closed the door behind him. It shut softly, and the room became more quiet. And intimate. An ache in her chest distracted her. She had to remind herself that this was only a business talk.

Then he strode across the room to take a seat in front of her desk, sitting back comfortably, his elbows resting against the sides of the upholstered chair. Jenny was suddenly made to realize that the guest chairs weren't meant for men his size. But with his hands on his thighs and his arms splayed to the side, he made himself look as comfortable as possible. He met her gaze and lifted the corners of his lips.

Gad, the man looked at ease in any situation. Well, she remembered Grace telling her about his former job in marketing for the electronics firm. Of course a marketing executive would be comfortable anywhere. And able to charm prospective customers. Able to charm her.

She drew her brows down and cleared her throat. 'Now, what is it you wanted to talk to me about?'

He took a minute before he spoke as his eyes traveled over her face. As if he were taking her measure. Then he leaned forward, one arm resting along the edge of the desk. There was a concerned look on his face.

'My mother can't eat chocolate.'

Jenny blinked. He had set up a special appointment just to tell her this? But she retained her professional demeanor, even though the closer he leaned, the faster her pulse danced, and the more her whole body trembled.

'Oh, I see,' she managed to say.

'Do you?'

It sounded like a challenge, but it was accompanied by a slight dropping of those sexy eyelids and a hint of a smile at the corners of his sensual mouth. She hadn't noticed just how sensual those lips were until now.

Stop that! she told her reckless mind. But she realized she had leaned forward a few more inches, hovering on the edge of her chair.

'Well, um, I understand that some of our residents have special diets. Is that what you mean?'

'Yes.'

Light began to dawn. 'You mean she can't eat chocolate in the dining room, and you'd like it taken off the menu?'

His sexy eyelashes drifted upward.

'I'm aware that you can't do away with chocolate entirely, but Mom tells me you've been serving chocolate cake or brownies almost every night for dessert. I wondered if you could change that.'

Jenny thought at that moment that she might change anything he asked. She swallowed. The sheer magnetism of the man had become so overpowering to her that Jenny envisioned herself getting down on her knees if he'd asked her to. *Sanity — where was her sanity?* Could she accuse him of sexual harassment? Make him stop?

'I'll, um, talk to the chef.'

Parker brought his other arm forward so that both his elbows leaned on the edge of the desk. He rested his chin on one folded fist. She had to fight an impulse to reach out and run her fingers through his thick, dark hair. Instead she clenched her fists in her lap.

'It seems to me,' Parker said, clearly enjoying himself, 'that it's just as easy to make white cake as chocolate cake.'

Then he changed his pose again and leaned back, hands folded in his lap again. He spoke with the same concern and authority as if he was negotiating a million-dollar deal.

'What about fruit pies?' he asked.

'What?'

'Can your baker manage fruit pies, or do you order them from outside?'

Jenny unconsciously leaned farther forward, her elbows on her desk and her hands folded. She didn't want him to be so far away.

'To be honest with you,' she told him, 'our baker isn't the greatest. We've had a lot of staff changes in the kitchen. But I will speak to him. I think he can do fruit cobblers.'

At an affordable cost, she almost added. But the financial problems of the place weren't any business of the residents or their families. On the contrary. She needed to keep their PR image intact to attract new residents. A full retirement home was the only way they could be profitable, assuming she could keep the doors open at all.

'Excellent,' Parker said with an air of approval. His eyes twinkled. 'I'll tell Mom she can look forward to more variety of desserts from now on.'

Jenny felt as if she'd just made it through a tough negotiation, but her opponent was so skillful that they'd both come out satisfied.

Only the trembling of her insides told her that she wasn't satisfied at all. Far from it. Drat. She must be still on the rebound from her breakup, just vulnerable enough to bounce into someone else's arms to reassure herself that she wasn't unwanted and unattractive.

Be that as it may, it was against her principles to take out her warped hunger on a family member of one of her residents. It could not be. If she couldn't maintain a business relationship with this group of people, she might lose her job. A job that might be lost anyway if her reduction of waste and economizing weren't enough to satisfy the head office.

And no doubt word of any philandering with residents' families would get back to corporate headquarters. The spy in the coffee klatch she was certain was reporting on her would get word to Mabel, the executive secretary at corporate. Somehow, Mabel always knew things before Jenny had time to report them.

But at this moment her hormones and body chemistry disagreed with her good sense. She backed away, sliding deeper into her executive swivel chair again.

Their business settled, he placed his hands on his muscular thighs and pushed himself to his feet.

'Sydney will be coming to the dining room with my mother.'

His demeanor changed suddenly from business tycoon to interested parent.

She nodded. 'Roger is tuning up in the commons. I'd better go rescue him and lock up the tuba. We'll join you at your table. I believe Grace has arranged the round table for five o'clock.'

At the mention of Grace's name, he grinned and his eyes softened. She would have missed it, but maybe it was because she hadn't gotten over staring at him that she saw it. Some light came into his eyes when she mentioned Grace.

That threw her. Was he aware that Grace was planning an assault on him? But of course he would be; the woman wasn't being very subtle. Jenny couldn't imagine the two of them together, and it stunned her to think he might actually be interested. Then, in the next instant, it annoyed her.

Maybe Parker had noticed Grace's interest and planned to take advantage of it for a quick one. Damn the man. She had known she needed to beware of his type. Too smooth. Probably got women to go to bed with him at the drop of a hat. But that he would take advantage of a woman like Grace angered Jenny. She stiffened her spine as she got up and walked around her desk.

He stood back to let her pass and then got to the door before her to open it.

'Thanks,' she said. But her icy demeanor was back in place.

'My pleasure,' came his soft, sexy voice.

Then his fingertips rested lightly on her back to guide her through the doorway as if they were going on a date instead of walking down the hall of a retirement center to find two children and the handsome escort's mother. It was just a polite gesture, and she was still burning with suspicion about this man's motives.

But her knees turned to pudding. She knew then that she would have to warn Grace to be on her guard. Parker McAllister was clearly dangerous to unwary single females.

4

A shock of warmth moved up Parker's arm when he guided Jenny out into the corridor. And with the surge of pure and simple sexual stimulation came the irony that the first woman he'd warmed up to in years was the ice queen who ran the retirement home. It would certainly look like he was angling for special favors if he made a pass at her. And making a pass was exactly what she made him feel like doing. Just watching her walk ahead of him down the hall sent a jolt of desire rushing through his body.

Her soft perfume, the lush ripples and the deep shade of her auburn hair, and the sway of her hips underneath the stirrup pants aroused the hunter instinct in him. Something he'd put on the back burner lately.

He'd been turned bitter by his ex-wife's grasping spirit and by the lean, hungry look he'd seen in the women who had noticed him lately. They all wanted a man for something. Jenny Knight didn't seem to want anything but order. With her clipboard, schedules and lists, she'd probably want to run a man's life the way the CEO at Millennium had run his.

He'd better get control of the sparks that were flying between them.

Confronted in the next moment with his mother and his daughter, his lustful thoughts receded to simmer silently, replaced by other concerns. He saw Roger talking to Sydney when they came out into the lobby and thought that was a good start. Both kids had been cleaned up and dressed in proper clothes for dinner. Roger wore a clean shirt and brown corduroy pants, and Sydney had put on a pink and white dress.

''Course I play other instruments,' Roger was telling her. 'I started on the trumpet a long time ago.' He made it sound passé. 'I played the baritone last year.'

'What's a berry tone?'

'It's like an F tuba, only smaller. It's for kids.'

'You're still a kid.'

Roger shoved his hands into his pockets, pushing his trousers further down his narrow hips.

'I'm in middle school now,' he said with superiority.

'When I get to middle school I'm going to play the bugle,' said Sydney.

'You mean the trumpet. Nobody plays the bugle.'

Parker observed Jenny's tight lips, and saw

the struggle evident on her pretty face. She must have felt the urge to intervene in her nephew's one-upmanship toward his little guest but wasn't sure how much good she could do.

Warning bells went off in Parker's head too. He was all too familiar with Sydney's tricks, and hoped she didn't take it into her head to goad the boy. But at their ages, rivalry was natural. He pulled his mouth to the corner, looking stern. But no one was paying him any attention.

Dorothy crossed the lobby to join them, a manilla folder under her arm. She was dressed in a soft plum outfit that complemented her white hair, and he noticed that she wore her favorite strand of pearls, a gift from Dad many years ago. She greeted Jenny and smiled at Parker. Something about the conspiratorial glint in his mother's blue eyes warned him that she had something up her sleeve. Then Jenny took hold of Roger's shoulder to propel him into the dining room. Parker took his mother's arm. Around them the voices of other residents going in to dinner added to the lively atmosphere.

Dorothy murmured into Parker's ear, 'What a nice little get-together this is, dear. It's good for you to have a chance to meet such nice women.'

'Mom,' he grunted, 'I had to come. We're all involved in this Christmas program.' He lifted his hands in a gesture of helpless surrender.

His mother gave an amused chuckle. 'I know, dear, but you never know. It *is* the season for *renewal*.'

He lifted a dark eyebrow at his mother's insinuation. Then he guided her into the carpeted dining room, separated into two halves by a free-standing fireplace in the center. A gas flame added holiday cheer, and the mantel was draped with cotton snow and a village scene. They steered a course through to the other side, where a round, circular table was set up in one corner. Floor-to-ceiling windows gave a view of the redwood deck and the bare apple trees beyond. In the distance the tiny headlights of cars were visible crossing the Cherry Creek dam road on this side of the reservoir.

He seated his mother and then got Sydney into a chair. Jenny and Grace seated themselves. Parker put on his affable face. Christmas still came with a sting of loss. Ironic, then, that he sold Christmas trees, something that brought cheer and Christmas spirit into a home. And now he was helping Sydney as representative of the children's choir. Christmas couldn't be easy on his mother either. Would they ever forget that Anna had left them just before Christmas time a year ago? The reminders were plentiful.

Andrei, a young Russian student in the black-and-white uniform of a waiter, came over to tell them what their choices were for the meal. They placed their orders without any complications, always a victory when kids were involved.

Jenny had on her professional face, and Parker realized he had chosen the seat opposite her. He could gaze all he wanted at her fine, straight nose, reddish-brown eyebrows and direct, brown eyes. Her shade of lipstick was a deep cinnamon. He wondered how it tasted.

After they had all been served hot drinks, Jenny began the discussion.

'Perhaps we can hear what Grace has planned for the program,' she said. 'Then we'll see if all the groups agree.'

'Do I have to listen?' asked Roger, generously lathering butter over his roll. 'I won't be here for the program.'

'No, you don't have to listen, Roger,' said Jenny. 'But it would be polite to do so. Besides, you might have some suggestions for us.'

Roger shoved his lips back and forth, as if considering.

'Where will the program be?' asked Sydney. She twisted her head twice, flicking her ponytails outward like fan blades.

Grace lifted an arm and pointed toward the deck outside the double glass doors. 'Out there in the plaza. An insulated tent will stretch across from the roofs, and a backdrop is being painted by my clever volunteers. The audience will be seated in the library downstairs and on the deck right there. There will be room for everyone.'

She gave Parker an exuberant smile. 'Of course, we might need some help with the shrubs.'

His attention was diverted from gazing at Jenny's exquisitely pink cheekbones.

'Shrubs?'

'Well,' she said, her eyelids closing and opening once, 'you are our shrub expert. It will be necessary for you to view the drawings for the stage setting, after which you might be able to advise us as to where to remove or trim shrubbery in preparation for the evening.'

'Grace,' said Jenny with slight irritation in her tone, 'we are not going to remove shrubs for this. We'd be denuded after the program.'

Parker quirked his lips in amusement. The opinionated Grace Douglas was giving Jenny a run for her money. It reminded him of his own former job, when he'd sometimes gotten stuck working with people someone else had hired. But the two women's sparring entertained him. The sort of program they ended up with hardly mattered to him. What mattered was that he was able to forget his personal life for a little while and help other people do things that mattered to them. And he was enjoying that. He was enjoying it very much.

'Well,' said Grace, far from giving up, 'if we're *denuded*, I'm sure Parker can do something about it.'

An exasperated sigh erupted from Jenny. 'He doesn't run a nursery, Grace. He sells trees only for the season.'

Grace shrugged her squarish shoulders in a gesture that reminded him very much of his late sister. It was endearing in its very forthrightness.

'Well. That's too bad.' Grace moved along, like the general she so resembled.

'Dorothy,' said Grace, turning her attention to the older woman, 'how is your committee coming along with the script?'

Dorothy's eyes gleamed. 'My committee is doing very well. Of course, the story's already been written for us, hasn't it? I mean, you can hardly change events recorded in the Scriptures. But we're making it accessible in modern language. And dividing it up for the readers.'

'Good, good,' said Grace. 'And have you decided what music you need where, and all of that?'

'We have,' said Dorothy. She smiled at her granddaughter. 'I'll show you where we'll pause in the dialogue and narration for music. Then Sydney can suggest some of the songs in her choir's repertoire.'

'Excellent.' Grace smiled all around at the little group. 'Then we are making great progress.'

Parker didn't miss the overt, suggestive look in Grace Douglas's wide green eyes. Her direct tactics amused him, but he suspected that they caused Jenny some consternation. Yet he could see how having such an enthusiastic steamroller might be valuable in a place like this, where programs kept the residents busy and active. As the meal was served, he had to hide a smile, wondering what Grace thought she was making great progress with.

He couldn't help feeling some tenderness for Grace's personality. But it was only because she was so like Anna that he felt he knew her. He didn't have any romantic inclinations in her direction. He liked her the way he would a friend.

As Andrei served their dinner, Jenny saw Parker's side glance at Grace and wondered for the second time if he might actually be interested in her. Dear Grace was a person all her own. She was obviously interested in Parker. And in true Grace Douglas fashion, she was going to promote her interests. It still surprised Jenny that Parker might return that interest, but she reaffirmed her resolve to make sure Grace knew what kind of a man she was considering getting involved with.

For herself, Jenny had already taken a stand, even if Parker's good humor and charming manners made her pulse sing. No dillydallying with a resident's son. The handsome, confident, Christmas-tree seller was off-limits for her. And dangerous for her program director as well.

She knew the pang in her heart was just more self-pity. Being left alone at the holiday season wasn't fun. And if she wasn't careful, her bah-humbug attitude would begin to show through her armor of professional cheerfulness. If her smiles didn't always reach her eyes, and if her good wishes weren't from the heart, she didn't want anyone to notice. She brought her mind back to their discussion.

'What about stage settings?' Jenny asked Grace. 'We have the small platform stage. I've budgeted for the rental of a sound system for one day. Will the readers use podiums?'

Grace waved a hand over Roger's head.

'The speakers will be seated in folding chairs behind the podium. When it's time to speak, all they have to do is get up and walk a few steps to the podium. That will work for your people, Dorothy, won't it?'

Dorothy nodded, set her fork down and patted the crumbs from her lips with a linen napkin.

'Of course. I'll give a complete script to each reader with their parts marked. My old typewriter still works. I should have no trouble typing everything up.'

'Excellent,' said Grace. 'Then we'll copy it in the front office.'

Grace turned to Sydney, who was mashing up her meatballs into the sauce of her stroganoff. 'How many songs do you think the choir would like to do?'

Sydney flicked her fork upright, sending a piece of meat across the table into Roger's lap.

'Hey,' he cried.

Sydney blinked innocently. Parker reached over and touched her arm.

'Careful of that fork, honey. You don't want

92

to catapult your food into Roger's plate.'

'Sorry,' Sydney said, wiggling her shoulders and looking down at her plate contritely.

Grace beamed at Parker. 'I see that you must be the great peacemaker in your family.'

Jenny saw Parker wince. Roger glowered, and she, herself, felt overcome with awkwardness. But Grace got the conversation back on track without missing another beat.

'So, how many songs do you think your group will want to do, dear?'

Sydney screwed up her mouth. 'We can do four, not counting the Christmas carols. Everybody should sing those.'

'Excellent,' replied Grace, digging into her meatballs with gusto.

Dorothy leaned forward. 'Do you want the script to indicate the entrances and exits for the animals?'

Jenny frowned. She had a bad feeling about those animals. You couldn't depend on live animals.

'Yes, yes,' agreed Grace, blotting her lips. 'I'll give the script to the animal trainers. They'll bring the trailers around behind the building, so there'll only be a short distance to go. It will be grand.'

Jenny caught Parker's lifted eyebrow, sharing the speculation that the plans sounded too elaborate. No wonder her friend was affected by him. He had the kind of charisma to make any woman shiver. And clearly he was as amused at the prospect of this full-scale production as she was anxious about it.

That caused Jenny another worry. Supposing he was planning to capitalize on Grace's suggestions about a shrub consultation and decided to take advantage of her then. She just couldn't imagine Parker taking Grace Douglas seriously, but he might not scruple at her throwing herself into his arms for a night.

Roger jolted Jenny out of her reverie. 'Can I go now?' he asked.

'Roger, the rest of us aren't finished. It isn't polite to leave the table before everyone else.'

His shoulders slumped. 'I have to warm up my instrument,' he told his plate of leftover food.

Jenny exhaled a breath. It was true that the music would start directly after supper as the residents gathered to finish trimming the tree.

'And I need to go get into my choir robe,' chirped Sydney. 'May I be excused, Daddy?'

Parker cast a warm look of empathy at Jenny. 'Perhaps we should let these two go, since they have to perform tonight.'

She nodded, mesmerized by his dark eyes. 'All right. Go on, kids. We'll see you in the commons room in a few minutes.'

The two kids rocketed out of their chairs and wound through the chairs and walkers in the dining room. Parker's dark-eyed glance still pinned Jenny to her chair, and she felt like squirming self-consciously. She turned her attention to Dorothy and Grace.

'All right, what else? Has the tent covering been ordered?'

'Yes, yes.' Grace nodded vigorously. 'All ordered. All the vendors have been con-tacted.'

'Good,' said Jenny. 'Oh, what about a rehearsal?'

The others looked at each other as if the idea had never occurred to them.

'Well,' said Grace, recovering quickly, 'a dress rehearsal with everyone would have to be on the same day, before supper. We can't afford to pay the animal trainers to come more than one time. And the tent and sound system only arrive that morning.'

'Then you'd better plan to rehearse that afternoon,' Jenny suggested. 'Two o'clock would do. And then everyone can rest and eat supper here before the program.'

Grace nodded thoughtfully. 'That will give everyone time to change into their costumes.'

Jenny finished her green beans. She would leave the costumes up to the rest of them, but she'd make darn sure the rehearsal went off without a hitch so there would be no surprises. There wasn't any room for surprises.

When their plates had been removed, they all got up to return to the commons room. Jenny couldn't help but notice Parker's impeccable manners as he helped his mother up and then took her hand in the crook of his arm. Very touching. But her ex had been charming that way as well. The problem was that Drake's manners and charm probably carried over to every woman he ever met, right into their bedrooms.

Oh my, thought Jenny wearily, realizing she was probably exaggerating. She just wanted to forget men for a while. She had planned to throw herself into work this holiday season to get over her self-pity. You just didn't have to have a man in your life all the time, she had reasoned. There were lots of single people in this world, she reminded herself stubbornly. Not everyone had a mate.

As she proceeded through the dining room, that thought niggled. Most of the elderly residents here were widowed or single, in fact. If they were lonely, at least they had each other for company now. Who did Jenny have in her life for company since she'd left Seattle?

Grace was a good friend, certainly, but as

96

much as Jenny liked her program director, she couldn't confide deep, private thoughts in her. She had to maintain some distance as the boss. She'd left other close friends behind in Seattle, and hadn't yet met many people here she'd bonded with. Those things took time, she'd told herself, cautioning herself to have patience in developing relationships.

But the glittering holiday decorations in the lobby made her realize just how alone she was this season. She was the head of an organization that served people, but her position left her alone. And she couldn't share the pressures of the job with anyone. Turn things around or the doors closed.

She had made it known in staff meetings that the balance sheet didn't look good and that she'd been hired to reduce waste and economize. None of the economies would affect the life or health of the residents, of course. But she had kept the keys to all the supply rooms and instituted tighter inventory measures.

'If we don't shape up the place,' she'd told them, 'we might not have a place to work in the future.' But none of them knew exactly how serious the situation was.

She felt an aching throb inside as she gazed at Parker's strong back. Was that how it had been for him at the top of a big electronics firm? Divorced and alone at the top? She wondered if perhaps that was why he'd chosen such a humble profession as selling Christmas trees. It brought him in contact with real people every day.

That must be it, Jenny realized. Parker must be getting his life back. As manager of a Christmas tree lot, he had a busy job, but he had time to balance his family life as well. His daughter got to spend time with him on weekends, and his mother was cared for here. But didn't he worry about money? Surely selling trees wasn't all he would ever do in life.

She saw the pride in Parker McAllister's eyes. Even if she was willing to give him the benefit of the doubt, he wouldn't be the kind of man to date a woman seriously when his own financial security was still at risk. And securing a future for his daughter should be first and foremost in his mind.

She'd better have a heart-to-heart talk with Grace; slow down her assault on the erstwhile executive. And apply some discipline to her own yearning hormones.

As she smiled and greeted the residents gathered now in the parlor and scattered around the commons room as well, her heart began to thaw. Everyone looked so bright and cheery in red and green and other holiday attire. Though it was against the rules for the staff to drink alcoholic beverages during working hours, wine was served for the party. She saw Parker wending through the residents, guests and arriving children's choir members. He held two plastic cups of wine high above the children's heads to avoid sloshing it on them.

'I don't normally drink on duty,' she quipped, gazing at the cup in his strong hand, 'but I guess this is a party.'

'Yes, it is,' he said, his eyes twinkling like warm coals. 'And we should toast to that.'

His eyes met and held hers, sending a shimmer inside her that matched the faint tinkling of bells she heard coming out of a box of decorations. It didn't do to be near this man, in spite of her resolves. They turned to watch Grace directing the residents in serious tree-trimming now.

'Your program director has quite a lot of enthusiasm,' said Parker.

Jenny was all too keenly aware of a small spurt of resentment and warning at his words.

'Yes, she does. I'm lucky to have her. It's her lack of experience I'm worried about.'

'How do you mean? Is this her first job in this capacity?'

'I wasn't referring to her work experience.'

Jenny's face burned with the obvious message she was sending, and Parker seemed to take the hint.

He turned back to melt her eyes with his own.

'What I meant,' he drawled slowly, indicating that he knew full well what she was conveying, 'was that she takes on ambitious projects with enthusiasm and competence. I wouldn't have minded having someone like her working for me in my previous occupation.'

'Is that so?' said Jenny.

She tried to read the flicker of emotion in his dark eyes as he sipped his wine. She wasn't sure if he was sorry he'd mentioned his former job. Still, the reference made her curious.

'What . . . ' She searched for the right phrase. 'What will you do when Christmas season is over?'

'You mean for work?'

'Yes. Um, Grace told me you'd parted from your former company.'

'Yes. It was something of a blessing. As to my plans, I'm not thinking about them until after the holidays.'

She watched his face as his eyes drifted to where his mother was helping with the decorations. Then she saw them light as

100

Sydney dashed into the room, white choir robe billowing. She skidded to a stop in front of the tall redheaded man who was now assembling the kids in the commons.

'The choir director?' she asked, following Parker's gaze.

'Hank DeVere. He's the music teacher at Sydney's school. Does a good job with kids.'

'You must be pleased about that.'

Parker tilted his head sideways and caught her gaze again.

'Yes. And what I meant about leaving my job is that it made me see some things I hadn't seen before.'

'Oh?' Now, why was she moved by the sincerity in those dark eyes?

He nodded. 'Like how important family is.'

She felt a pang of regret at that. 'You're lucky to have them here.'

'Do you have any family nearby? Besides your nephew, I mean.' His look was so full of concern, it threw Jenny off balance.

'Well, my sister is usually here, but not this year. My parents live in Seattle. I couldn't make it back to see them this time. My grandmother isn't living. She spent her last years here at Cherry Valley. It's why I . . . try to do a good job here.'

Those thickly lashed lids lowered just a fraction. What did she see there that she

101

wasn't reading? Something a little sad. It confused her, sent a dizzy spiral through her middle.

'I'm sorry,' he said, 'that you couldn't be with your folks for Christmas.'

'It's okay,' she said, hearing the resignation in her voice. 'After all, it's not a tragedy.'

Christmas isn't fun, she wanted to shout. Careful, careful. She could not in any way intimate to him that the retirement home was in trouble. She was distracted by Roger, who was dragging the tuba across the wood floor.

Sydney stepped up between Roger and the music director and introduced them as Jenny watched from where she and Parker stood in the parlor.

To Parker, she said, 'It's just too bad my sister had to rush off to help her aunt-in-law in Maine.'

'And leave you with Roger.'

'Well, yes.' She shook her head. 'It's not that I don't enjoy Roger. I do. But I hadn't planned on having to take care of him just now.'

Another sip of wine was in order, and she took it to steady her nerves.

His expression was quizzical. Then a warm light spread across his face.

'Listen, if you need someone to help keep Roger busy, I might have an idea. Think he'd like a weekend job?'

Jenny's eyes opened wider at the prospect of Roger working. Should she feel guilty or relieved at the thought of occupying some of Roger's time with productive labor? This must be another insight coming from an experienced parent who obviously had thought out his philosophy of child rearing thoroughly.

'Well, I don't know. He is supposed to do his music lessons and homework. But he might like that.'

Then she wrinkled her brow. 'But legally, he's too young to get paid to work for a business.'

'I can pay him with a gift certificate to his favorite store. If his parents approve, of course.'

'No question there. Maureen would be thrilled. I'm sure of it.'

She looked at him a little guiltily. Did it sound like she was too eager to get rid of Roger? Well, wasn't she? It would be hard enough to coordinate their schedules during the school week. Parker McAllister just went up a notch in her estimation. Maybe he did have a few redeeming qualities.

'You must really like kids,' she said.

He looked a little regretful. 'Well, I don't see enough of Sydney. I guess I'm overdoing it, now that I have the time. I used to travel a lot for my job. That gets old.'

They sipped their wine contentedly, and she was aware that the fuzzy feelings in her brain were turning into dangerous thrums of desire. She didn't miss the way Parker's eyes glanced at her chest now and then, but then hid his gaze under those lowered lashes. She suddenly imagined what it would feel like to have those large, confident hands brush across her breasts. She had to shut her eyes and breathe deeply to push the fantasy away.

When she opened them again, Parker was gazing casually at the crowd. If he was having similar lustful thoughts, he wasn't giving anything away. She tried to straighten out her thoughts and concentrate on the idea he'd suggested.

If Parker took Roger off her hands for part of the weekend, that would leave her more free time. Hadn't she just been telling herself that she had lots to do in her office? And she had a long list of errands to run on Saturday, when the post office, the dry cleaner, the hardware store and the health food store were open. A sudden vision of Parker and the kids at the Christmas tree lot made her feel envious. They'd be having fun while she either buried herself in paperwork or stood in a long line at the post office to mail her packages back home.

Stop feeling sorry for yourself, Jenny Knight, she admonished herself. She had known this season would be difficult. She just had to stiffen her resolve to get through it. And not be so foolish as to lap up the attention that the handsome and charming Parker McAllister was dispensing in her direction.

'Don't let me keep you from mingling with the residents,' Parker said in a warm tone, interrupting her thoughts.

He had leaned his head closer, so that his breath fanned her hair. His velvety voice spiraled into her ear and set off a vibrating frequency inside her already weakened limbs. Better put down the wine, she thought. She was too much under the influence already. Or under his influence, perhaps.

'Thanks. I'd better do my share of the decorating.'

Out of the corner of her eye, Jenny saw that Roger had gotten settled in a chair with a music stand to the left of the choir. A plump woman in a blue and silver holiday sweater and skirt spoke with the music director and then with Roger. She crossed to the piano and then played a note. Jenny heard a similar pitch, several octaves lower, emanate from the tuba. The accompanist sounded the note again, and Roger rumbled in tune.

'That's a lovely reindeer, Mrs. Owen,' Jenny commented to one of the oldest ladies.

The elderly woman turned and smiled at her. 'It reminds me of something I used to have as a child.'

Jenny watched her place the decoration carefully on a tree branch. The tree was lovely and full. And with each decoration that went up on it, it seemed to swell with beauty. Jenny was suddenly glad that Parker had brought them such a lovely tree. It almost made her want one in her own apartment. But that was silly. She wasn't going to decorate just for herself. And Roger would have his own tree at home when his parents got back. If they got back in time for Christmas . . . Here was another worry that crept into her mind, but she couldn't think about that now. It did remind her, however, that she hadn't bought Roger a present yet.

Behind her in the commons, the music got under way. 'Jingle Bells,' 'Oh, Christmas Tree' and 'The Holly and the Ivy' didn't sound bad coming from children's voices, accompanied by the piano, with the oompahs of the tuba booming on first and third beats. Roger was really pretty good for a kid his age, she guessed.

She made a few more encouraging remarks

to the tree decorators and then circled the room. The music and the general joviality seemed to increase the gaiety, and voices rose to continue the din of conversation around the tree. After one more song, the kids took a break.

Sydney careened across the floor and into her dad.

'Ho, there, kiddo,' he said, leaning down to pat her back. 'That was good. Are you doing any more?'

'Oh, yes,' said Sydney. 'This is only a break. I need a drink of water.'

Parker and Sydney moved off in the direction of the refreshments and Jenny got distracted by making sure all of the delicate, breakable decorations made it out of their tissue wrappings and onto the tree without mishap. In a few more minutes the kids were back and everyone reassembled. She was aware of exactly where Parker took up a position on the other side of the fireplace, from which he could evidently see everything. Like a king observing people for whom he was responsible. His face looked beneficent, and oh, so sexy.

In the commons room, Roger lugged the tuba toward himself and spread his knees apart to balance it upright. The director raised his baton and the accompanist in blue and silver turned her head to wait for the downbeat.

Down came the baton. The accompanist struck the piano keys and Roger blew on his mouthpiece. But a very muted tone was all that came forth. Jenny saw Roger frown, take a breath and then press his face up against the huge mouthpiece once more. Again the nearly nonexistent, muted tone.

Jenny stopped, hand lifted with a decoration, watching as Roger scooted off his chair, lowered the tuba and looked into the bell of the instrument.

The angelic faces of the choristers became distracted by Roger's poking his arm into the bell of the tuba. Their voices died away, and the director tapped the baton on the music stand to regain their attention.

But Roger glowered at the front row, his arm still fishing inside the long bell.

Jenny put down the decoration in her hand and stepped forward, sensing an incident and wanting to prevent it before it happened.

'Is everything all right?' she asked as she crossed the wood floor toward Hank Devere, the music teacher.

She heard heavy footsteps, and realized that Parker was on her heels.

'No,' grumbled Roger, lightning bolts erupting from his narrowed brown eyes.

Jenny noticed that Sydney had buried her face in her music book and was trying to disappear behind two other little girls. Parker strode across to them.

Roger finally pulled a long red sock out of the bell and brandished it for everyone to see as he glared at Sydney.

'She put a sock in my tuba,' he said.

5

Horror coursed through Jenny as she reached for the sock, desperate to prevent any more chaos from erupting. She caught the look of consternation on Parker's face as he struggled with mirth. But then he stepped forward and reached a long arm into the group of children, who had burst into cackles of laughter at Roger's expense.

'Sydney,' boomed his powerful voice.

'Yes, Daddy,' came a muffled squeak.

'Come here, miss. I want to ask you a question.'

The other robed children parted for Sydney to step through. From the way she gazed at her father, with lowered head, Jenny knew she had some discipline coming. But she also caught the self-satisfied gleam in Sydney's eyes as she darted a look at Roger.

Jenny recognized this as a declaration of war. Little Sydney had won the first confrontation. Well, she'd had a feeling that an eight-year-old girl and an eleven-year-old boy might be a bad mix.

Parker folded himself down to squat at eye level to Sydney. He didn't touch her, but his penetrating gaze finally forced her head up to meet his eyes.

'Did you do it?' he asked.

Her left shoulder came up in a shrug, and she nodded her head up and down.

'Very well. Now, see how you've disrupted the program.'

'I saw the sock lying on the floor,' Sydney explained to her father. 'There was the tuba. There was the sock. I just sort of did it.'

'Thanks for telling us, Sydney. You're going to have to apologize to Roger.'

Sydney looked at the older boy in revulsion. 'Why? He's snotty. He said I was just a little kid and that girls were stupid.'

'Roger,' exclaimed Jenny. 'Did you say that?'

'Did not,' he said, hands on hips, glaring at Sydney.

'Did so,' she retorted, her own hands on her hips as she turned to face him.

Parker stood up. 'All right, that's enough. We aren't going to get into a shouting match here. This is a music program. Sorry, Hank. Can you pick up where you left off?'

Jenny groaned inwardly. Out of the corner of her eye, she tried to judge just how much the interruption had caught the attention of the residents by the tree. Mr. Saito was sitting in a wing chair, watching them from the

111

parlor. From the way he smiled slyly, she felt a tingle at the base of her neck. Could he be spying on her? She narrowed her eyes slightly at Mr. Saito, who nodded, his hands resting on the crook of his cane.

'We'll talk about this later,' she said to Roger, following him back to his chair. 'Just go ahead and finish the program.'

He stared at her grumpily. 'Girls shouldn't be so bossy about what everyone's going to do in the big Christmas program.'

'Really?' she replied. 'I thought you weren't planning to be here then.'

His eyelids came down to veil his eyes, but she sensed his own doubt that he'd be able to go home for Christmas. She felt a stab of sympathy. How boring for Roger to be cast adrift at a retirement home with an aunt who didn't know how to care for boys. She suddenly stopped thinking about her own problems and considered what it must be like for him.

Her lips parted at this realization. She turned and nearly collided with Parker, who caught her arm and pulled her aside so the music could get under way. She couldn't help leaning into the circle of his arm as he slid it behind her, then quickly ceased touching her. Still, his shoulder was angled behind hers, and for a moment, she drank in that warm support. Here was a man who seemed to know what to do with children. It was a skill she was quickly coming to admire.

He glanced at her, and her face felt flushed.

'You handled that very well,' she said in a hushed tone, trying to recover.

They were standing by the wall, out of the way of the commotion. If any of the other residents had noticed the altercation between the kids, they gave little sign. They just continued with their decorating, their merriment punctuated now and then by Grace's bursts of loud laughter.

Parker's eyes smiled, though his lips remained closed. 'Rivalry,' he said. 'Kids that age will goad each other.'

'Yeah, I guess.' Jenny shook her head. 'I guess I'm ill-prepared to make the holidays pleasant for my nephew.'

His gaze was sympathetic and thoughtful. 'I know how you feel.'

Some new emotion edged into her heart, and she wondered if he was thinking that the holidays for Sydney might be strained, with two different households to try to be a part of. Her heart warmed with a sense of camaraderie, and an achiness that she didn't quite recognize as longing. Hers and Parker's circumstances were different, but they shared a resonance.

In the next moment she tried to discipline her maudlin sentimentality. Why did the holidays have to be so darned emotional? They were meant to cheer everybody up. Instead, if you had loss in your life, it became all the more poignant at this time.

She allowed herself one more look at Parker's handsome profile, resisting the urge to move closer. His thick hair was so tempting. What would it feel like to brush it across his brow?

'I'd better get over there,' she said, nodding to the tree decorating. 'Do my part, you know.'

The choir was performing another song, and for some reason, Jenny thought that Roger's oompahs sounded louder. So loud, they drowned out the voices in spots. She must be standing too close.

Parker grinned at her. 'Since we averted a disaster over here, I'll join the party as well.' He nodded toward the parlor.

They separated and Jenny mingled with the residents and staff for the next forty-five minutes. Then she went to the kitchen to check with the supervisor, Mini, to make sure they had enough table waiters for tomorrow. Staff turnover was a problem. It was hard to find good employees, and not many of them wanted to work for long in a retirement home. Students and young people wanted upward mobility, and there wasn't that much to offer them here if they didn't have patience and a real desire to serve.

And Jenny would not employ lazy wait staff. She watched the dining room, timing how quickly they served the meals. She knew they thought she was a tyrant, but she had to do it. It was one more exercise in reducing waste and toeing the bottom line.

Then she went into her office to go over a classified ad they were placing in the newspaper to recruit more staff. Before she knew it, the music had stopped, and she heard voices in the lobby.

The children were leaving. Jenny joined Grace in thanking the redheaded music teacher. Grace was pumping Hank DeVere's hand up and down. Jenny thanked the children and parents. But Parker and Sydney were nowhere to be seen.

There were fewer residents in the parlor now, just a few elderly men and women sitting quietly looking at the tree. Their wrinkled faces hid whatever emotion the Christmas tree brought to them. Were they remembering long ago, happier Christmases? The same stab of resentment that Christmas wasn't a happy time for everyone pierced Jenny's heart. Mightn't it be better for some if they could just ignore the holidays altogether?

She saw no sign of Dorothy McAllister either, and assumed that Parker had taken his mother and daughter back to her apartment. Well, there was no reason to see him again this evening. In fact, it would be better if she didn't. His warmth and charisma were becoming dangerous, and she recognized her own vulnerability. If he did show up at her door, looking at her with those melancholy brown eyes, she wouldn't trust her powers to resist inviting him in. But in the next second she told herself to stop dreaming.

She had recognized the pride in Parker McAllister's face, had read his wariness of women. A man of his caliber without a secure income wasn't going to pay serious court to a woman in her position. He might be able to get away with a one-night stand with some women, but he would know better than to try that with the general manager of his mother's retirement home.

She rounded up Roger, who had packed his tuba in the soft leather case.

'All set?' she asked.

'Yeah.'

Again there was the problem of transporting the heavy instrument back to Jenny's apartment. She reached down and tugged on the handle. It was heavy, but she was taller than Roger and so more able to manage it. No wonder he had commandeered a rolling cart, even though he really shouldn't have.

'This thing is pretty heavy,' she said. 'How do you usually get it from place to place?'

'In a car.' His expression told her that hers was a stupid question.

'Oh, I see. Well, come on.'

'I'm hungry.'

She set the tuba back on the floor. 'Didn't you finish your dinner?'

He rolled his eyes. 'That was hours ago.'

'Oh. What are you hungry for now?'

'Pizza.'

Jenny had no idea whether feeding a child pizza at night was good for his digestion or sleep. But she had to think of something.

'Tell you what — let's go to the kitchen. They don't have pizza in there, but maybe we can make you a sandwich.'

Roger followed her into the kitchen. The staff had all gone home, but she knew her way around well enough to get out what was needed. After setting sliced turkey, ham, mayonnaise, lettuce, tomato, pickles and bread on the counter, she handed Roger a bread knife.

'Why don't you make it?'

Roger set to until the sandwich was stacked up high. Then Jenny got him a plate and led him into a corner of the dining room to eat it.

Not wanting to sit and stare at him while he devoured the sandwich, Jenny circled the dining room and wandered into the far, darkened portion of the room. She paused beside the picture windows, looking out at the deck. This half of the dining room was dark enough that she could see out to the shadowy deck and the starry sky beyond the roof line. A clear, dark night sky revealed twinkling stars. A pretty sight.

She heard a board creak outside and tried to penetrate the darkness on the deck with her eyes. Movement drew her attention to a silhouetted figure. Her heart jumped. A tall, broad-shouldered man was standing there. Parker?

She moved toward the doors, and although she only had on her sweater for warmth, she pushed through to the chilly deck. He turned at her approach, and she stopped, seeing her breath condense on the cold night air.

'Hi,' she said.

'Hi,' he returned. 'I hope I didn't frighten you.'

'No, no. I was just . . . looking at the stars, and I thought I saw someone out here. I thought someone might have gotten locked out.'

He crossed the redwood boards of the

118

deck. 'Are you cold? Take my jacket.'

He peeled off his soft, black fleece jacket and dropped it across her shoulders. She snuggled into its warmth, enjoying the male feel that came along with it.

'Thanks. I can only stay here for a minute. Roger's eating a sandwich inside.'

'I wanted to see you anyway,' he said.

Her heart leapt. But his next words brought her back down to earth.

'I wanted to make sure your nephew's ego wasn't too bruised.'

He stood close, as if he wanted to protect her from the cold air with his own body warmth. She hugged herself, trying to retain as much body heat as she could inside the jacket, knowing she couldn't stay out here for long. At night in December, the temperature dropped substantially. But her shivering was only partly from the cold.

'I think he's all right. At least he's being well-fed.'

Parker moved a little closer, as if he might move his arm to cross her shoulders, but he kept his hands in his pockets. They both looked out at the distant stars.

'Lovely sky, isn't it?' she said.

With Parker standing beside her, she felt more appreciative of such simple beauties. The chemistry between them was resonating again, and the hesitation in his answer made her wait intently for what he was going to say.

'Yeah. Makes me think of my sister. We lost her last year.'

A stab of shock coursed through Jenny. From the way he said it, the meaning was clear. 'Oh, my. I didn't know. I'm sorry.'

'Thanks. I guess Mom didn't mention it.'

'No, she didn't.'

She should have known, though. Something so significant happening to a family was bound to affect it in many ways. Jenny was stunned.

Parker waited thoughtfully for a moment, and she certainly wasn't about to trespass on his thoughts.

'My sister had leukemia. In the end, her death was a release from the pain. But it's still hard.'

Jenny rocked with surprise and sympathy for him. Her own problems seemed insignificant in light of this. Here was another traveler through life for whom the holidays could only bring pain, and the anguish touched her heart. Before she knew what she was doing, she reached out and touched his arm.

'I understand.'

He glanced down at her hand, and she removed it self-consciously. But he didn't move away.

'I know it's hard for any of us to understand what someone else goes through,' she stumbled on. 'I just mean I'm sorry I didn't know.'

He shook his head, looking out at the sky again, as if trying to fathom infinity.

'I believe she's gone on to the next life,' he said. 'But you still can't help but feel regret for all the things you should have done for someone like that.'

Self-recrimination was evident in his words, and she was startled by his depth of feeling. Had she misread him?

A sudden spurt of grief touched her heart. Not only was this man a divorced parent without a real job, he had a personal loss to deal with that was still raw. It made her wonder how he coped. Thinking about Dorothy in light of the fact that the woman had lost a grown child gave her pause.

'Dear me,' she said aloud. 'There's so much about my residents I guess I don't know.' And had been too busy adding numbers to learn.

He sighed, gazing at the stars wistfully. 'You know, it's funny: Sometimes I feel I can communicate with my sister.'

Embarrassment rushed through her, and she stepped away. 'I'm sorry. I shouldn't have interrupted your thoughts. I'll leave you alone.'

'No, don't,' he said quickly. 'I mean, I like the company.'

Their hearts in tune, Jenny stayed beside him for a moment longer. The crisp night air was redolent with the scent of someone's wood fire and the hint of snow. The sounds of cars in the distance reminded her of the unceasing life of the sprawling city. But most of all, she felt Parker's inner spirit reach out and touch hers. It was hard to explain. In that moment, they shared something she couldn't name. With regret, she felt the tug of her nephew, eating his way through the late-night snack in the dining room.

And the fact that they shouldn't be out here together for this long anyway. The spy might be watching. And she could just imagine the wagging tongues of residents with windows facing this deck.

'I should go in,' she said, still rooted to the spot.

Parker half turned toward her, his face hovering near hers. Jenny's heart danced high in her chest. They were only inches apart. It felt as if he was going to kiss her. But then she realized the inappropriateness of that and lowered her head, steadying herself against the railing and stepping away.

'I . . . I'm glad you told me,' she said.

He didn't say anything, didn't have to. He

just watched her as she moved away. Then he followed to open the door for her, and they both stepped inside.

★ ★ ★

An unfamiliar warmth pervaded Parker as he followed Jenny inside. He could swear he had been about to kiss her. But it had been so unexpected. One minute he was telling her about Anna, and the next he'd reacted to Jenny's hand reaching out to console him. He didn't want sympathy, never had. But in that moment he had wanted whatever it was she had to offer.

The fact that his dear sister was gone, and that his personal life was a mess, had been his own damned business for so long, the concept of sharing had not been an option. He wasn't used to anyone else caring, in any case. Anyone but Mom, who worried about him incessantly. And about whom he felt guilty because he didn't spend enough time with her and could never make up to her for the loss of Anna.

Life in recent years had been a series of stresses, and Parker had taken the Christmas tree lot because he wanted to do something simple for a change. Damn the corporations. But Jenny Knight was beginning to get under

123

his skin. Standing out there in the cold night air, he'd felt like she'd been able to read his mind. It was a totally unnerving experience.

He shook his head as he watched her take Roger's plate and return it to the kitchen. The young man stared up at him as he wiped a napkin across his mouth, removing most of the mustard smeared on his cheeks.

Parker relaxed. He was at home with boys this age, knew how to talk to them.

'Say, young man, how would you like a job for a few hours this weekend?'

Roger gazed at him suspiciously. 'Doing what?'

'Helping me at my Christmas tree lot. I need someone to help take care of customers and explain prices. It might be a way for you to earn money for something you've been wanting to buy.'

That got Roger's attention, just as Jenny returned from the kitchen.

Roger's eyes slid toward his aunt. 'Like a new football?'

Parker grinned. 'That could be arranged.'

'Wow. Mom won't let me play football at school.' He made a face. 'Too dangerous. But if I had my own, I could practice throwing passes at home.'

Roger got up from the table, his eyes wide behind his glasses.

'All right, then,' said Parker. 'I'll pick you up after your music lesson tomorrow.'

He glanced at Jenny, whose face was rosy from the winter air. What was it about her that bewitched him so? He regretted that they'd been interrupted, and for a moment, he let a fantasy run away with him. In his mind's eye, he took her head in his hands and then cupped her face for a kiss. His eyes dwelled for a moment on those bright lips, and when he met the spark in her eye and noticed her shallow breathing, his male instinct told him she was feeling the same way. They stared breathlessly at each other for only a moment before Roger interrupted.

'We going now?'

'Yes, son,' Parker said, coming to himself. 'We're going.'

He escorted them back to pick up the tuba. When he saw Jenny lift it, he immediately reached for the heavy bag.

'I'll carry that,' he said.

'It's not really necessary.'

'I wouldn't be a gentleman if I didn't offer to carry it back to your apartment for you.'

Jenny had a mischievous gleam in her eye. 'We could always commandeer a utility cart.'

Roger rolled his eyes at her. 'You said I couldn't do that anymore.'

'I said you should ask someone before you

did it,' Jenny retorted. 'I spoke to the head housekeeper during the party and checked out a cart. We now have a cart assigned to us for the duration of your visit.'

Roger studied her somewhat dubiously, but Jenny led them across the lobby and then marched toward the corridor leading to the apartments. She stopped at a door, which she unlocked with a key that dangled from her wrist. In a few seconds, she rumbled out a gray rectangular, two-level cart with four wheels. Parker hoisted the tuba onto the top.

'I'm going back to Mom's anyway,' he said. 'I'll walk you part way.'

Jenny beamed at him, looking almost playful. He thought she might be in a good mood because she was beginning to get a handle on how to take care of her nephew. Or could it be that she'd been pleasantly stimulated by their near kiss? Parker felt his own foolish look of enjoyment at being with them as he followed Jenny down the corridor.

They parted at the stairwell. She turned to wave.

'Thanks,' she called back, as her little procession took the turn by the small seating area and headed for the back wing.

He lifted a hand, wishing he was accompanying them. But to what end? He needed to get Sydney home to bed and to carry on with his life. A life he had vowed didn't need a woman in it. Or maybe that didn't need just any woman.

As Parker took the stairs to the third floor two at a time, some rattled thoughts bounced around in his head. He'd never considered himself a romantic. And after his divorce, then Anna's death, he'd shied away from any close relationships. It would be suicide to take one on right now, while he was shifting and sifting his own life around to find a different way to live. Too bad his aching groin and a sudden hunger for more of Jenny Knight's gentle touch was interfering with his stoic resolve.

6

Jenny half awoke Saturday morning but still remained in her dream. A dark, handsome face hovered above her in her semiwakeful state, sensual lips only inches from her own, eyes gazing dreamily down at her. She stared at his wide, strong cheekbones and dark lashes and eyes, her hand drifting toward his naked shoulder.

With a purr of sensual pleasure, Jenny realized that her dream had them naked together between soft sheets. She felt his strong torso, her hands on his firm, tautly muscled stomach.

She squeezed her eyes shut, clinging to the receding dream as the morning forced its way into her consciousness. She lifted a hand to press against her hot forehead, aware of a deep ache of desire. Then she emitted a long, exasperated groan and shook her head.

She mumbled to herself as she threw the covers aside to cool off her overheated body and got up. Grunting to herself, she pulled her fingers through tangled auburn hair.

'As moon-eyed as Grace,' she said to herself as she stumbled to the bathroom.

She made coffee while Roger got dressed and then escorted him to the dining room for breakfast. He busied himself with a pile of pancakes while Jenny stopped to greet the elderly breakfasters.

'I'll grocery shop today so we can eat in the apartment,' she told him when she sat down to some scrambled eggs. 'Is there anything you'd particularly like?'

'Pizza.'

'I'll buy some frozen pizza, but you can't eat that as a steady diet.'

'Why not?'

She sighed. 'Doesn't Maureen ever talk to you about nutrition?'

He jerked his shoulders up and down in a quick shrug. 'Do you like seafood?'

Jenny lifted her brows and tilted her head slightly. 'Why, yes.'

Whereupon Roger opened his mouth and exposed his chewed-up food on a stretched-out tongue for her to 'see food.'

'Roger! Shut your mouth.'

He chewed and swallowed, his clever glint conveying the fact that he had one up on her.

'Those are not acceptable manners for this dining room,' she chastised. 'Or for any dining room, for that matter. What you do at home is your business, but while you're living

129

with me, you will behave like a gentleman. Understood?'

She realized she was being a disciplinarian, but she wasn't going to back down. The only way she could get through the holiday season with Roger underfoot would be to make sure little incidents like last night's sock in the tuba were not repeated. Roger would have to mind his *p*s and *q*s while under her roof.

She looked around surreptitiously to see if any of the breakfasters were watching them, and thought she saw a few amused smiles, but no one's eyes gave away whether they'd seen his little demonstration.

From across the room, she caught a glimpse of Dorothy McAllister's hand lifted in a cheerful wave. Jenny nodded to her. She would swear there was mischievous speculation in those shining blue eyes. It made Jenny's cheeks warm to think that she'd just been fantasizing about Dorothy's son.

Jenny averted her eyes. She'd already drawn the lines. Parker wasn't jeopardizing a job if he moved in for a pass at her; she was. She risked another glance at Dorothy, who was still looking at her.

'Can we have hamburgers for dinner?' Roger's voice interrupted her thoughts.

'What?'

'If you're shopping, can you buy hamburger?'

'Yes, I'll buy some lean hamburger. You'll be plenty hungry after working today.'

She half expected Roger to make a face at the mention of work, but he only gazed from her to the syrup he was mopping up with his last bite of pancake. Well, maybe Parker was right. Maybe kids did enjoy helping out.

She suddenly wondered if that was what troubled Parker. If Sydney had grown up with his ex-wife, maybe Parker worried that his daughter would grow up spoiled. Maybe that was why he had Sydney help him at the tree lot too.

Uh oh, Jenny thought so loud, she was afraid she'd spoken. Parker would have both Sydney and Roger at the lot. Wasn't he worried that the two of them together would be trouble? Or was he still interested in improving their manners?

'Come on,' she said when Roger was finished. 'Time to get you to your music lesson.'

She paused, halfway out of her seat. 'Do we take the tuba with us? Or is there one at the teacher's that you can use?'

'I just have to take my mouthpiece,' he said, sliding out of the chair.

'Well, that's a blessing.'

After a quick stop at the apartment, she loaded Roger into her dark blue Volkswagen Jetta. They made trivial small talk as she followed his directions to the teacher's house, surprised at how she felt. Her irascibility of the previous few days had been replaced by a more optimistic outlook. She really didn't mind taking Roger to the lesson. She'd be able to get the grocery shopping done while he huffed and puffed for his instructor, and then she could get him back home in time for Parker to pick him up.

Parker, Parker, Parker. Was that the cause of this unfamiliar lightness of heart? If so, she'd better beware. That way lay danger and disaster, especially now, when she had to concentrate so hard on work.

Fifteen minutes later, she strolled up and down the aisles in the nearby grocery store. She enjoyed shopping for healthy food for Roger and herself to eat. He would still get his hamburger and pizza, but he would also get plenty of vegetables, brown rice, fruit and lentil soup. How much more interesting shopping was when you weren't just cooking for yourself. But who else was it that she was beginning to fantasize cooking for?

She studied a packet of Mediterranean herb seasoning mix used to prepare sautéed tofu. *Put it back*, her conscience said. *You know Roger wouldn't like sautéed tofu.* She turned the packet over, reading the serving suggestions.

A romantic dinner for two can be created by . . .

Put it back, she warned herself again.

'It doesn't have to be a romantic dinner,' she mumbled to the packet. She could make it for herself and keep the leftovers for lunch.

'Do you always talk to seasoning packets?'

The deep, familiar voice jolted her so that she swung her arm around and knocked it right into her shopping cart, which rolled a few inches. He reached behind her to catch it.

There was Parker McAllister again, appearing beside her as if he'd just been conjured out of a magic lantern. He looked his usual sexy self in a red plaid shirt peeking out of the v-neck of a thick navy sweater. His jeans fit his hips like a snug second skin.

'You okay? I'm sorry if I startled you.'

'It's okay. I just didn't see you.'

She grasped the cart and tossed the packet into it to land on her other purchases. His dark eyes glanced at her elbow.

'You sure you didn't hurt yourself?'

'Uh, yeah, sure.'

The concern in his eyes chiseled at her armor. Then his gaze transmuted into the humor she found so appealing and so disconcerting at the same time.

'I think I interrupted your conversation with that seasoning mix you so casually cast aside,' he said.

She knew he was teasing her, and she ought to resent it. But somehow Parker McAllister teased in a way that got beneath her firmest resolve. The ease with which he inhabited any surroundings impinged on her, and she realized what it was. He was comfortable wherever he was. He wasn't intimidated or ill at ease with anyone that she had seen.

While she dug for an appropriate answer, she felt a change wash through her. After their conversation last night, she'd grudgingly admitted that he must not be the callous ne'er-do-well she'd first assumed him to be. There was a tenderness about him that was hard to ignore. Was she getting sentimental?

A tug of emotion spread through her. Joking with Parker McAllister in the grocery store aisle seemed like what she'd rather be doing than anything else on earth. Then she sobered. There was too much else on earth that she had to be doing. She couldn't be wasting time here, as pleasant as it might seem.

He still looked at her expectantly, and she glanced self-consciously at the packet in the cart. It had fallen with the back side up, recommending the romantic dinner. His eyes strayed in that direction and then he reached for it.

'Oh, Mediterranean tofu. I make a mean tofu stir fry.'

'You do? I've never tried it.'

He erased a dreamy expression from his face with some regret. He replaced the packet in her cart.

'Sorry. I didn't mean to keep you from your shopping,' he said.

His own shopping basket was half-full behind her.

'Oh, it's all right. Do you shop here often?'

'Sometimes. It's close to Mom's, you know.'

'Of course.'

And where do you live? her disobedient mind wanted to know.

He put his large hands on his own shopping cart, which was full of fresh produce, a few packaged meats and cereal boxes. He must be cooking for Sydney, or someone else. That thought niggled.

'I'm taking advantage of the time Roger is at his music lesson to shop,' she said. 'My sister didn't give me any warning when she dropped him off, so I need to stock up now.'

'I know what you mean.'

'Well, I'd better finish up and get him so I can get back to the apartment. Shall I have him ready for you in the lobby at eleven-thirty? He does seem to be looking forward to it.'

Something flashed in those deep brown eyes. 'The lobby will be fine.'

And it would be more appropriate, Jenny thought, remembering that she couldn't risk having people see Parker coming to her apartment.

'The lobby, then.'

She turned to push her cart along, and he smiled at her before pushing his in the opposite direction.

There were depths to the man she hadn't plumbed, no doubt about it. But she knew she'd be a fool if she decided to plumb them. Her job was on the line. What crackled between them would just have to be put on hold. For another lifetime.

★　★　★

Parker had seen Jenny's look of embarrassment when he'd picked up the seasoning mix. So, she was planning a romantic dinner for two, was she? He wondered who the lucky man was before he forced the thought from his mind. Whom Jenny Knight dated was no business of his. Though the heat that warmed his body when he saw her was undeniable. And the way he couldn't stop teasing her was another response he needed to learn to curb.

She was laced up so tight. He wondered why she was so stern and driven. Sure, it would be a challenge to run a place like Cherry Valley. But she ran it with such an iron fist, he wondered how she could possibly enjoy her job. Jenny Knight needed to loosen up.

He wondered devilishly if his mom's coffee klatch knew anything about Jenny's social life. He was quite aware of Dorothy's little circle of friends at the retirement home. Not a thing went on there that missed their keen observation. But he wasn't going to ask, no siree.

He waited in the vitamin aisle until Jenny checked out. They were both conscious of something going on between them. He'd seen her tremble when he gazed down at her. But he was determined to control his own reactions, even if the chemistry between them was reaching sizzling point. She'd hardly be interested in a man who was minimally employed, with a daughter to support. Smart woman. And he knew that for him to make a pass at Jenny would have to mean something more serious than an invitation to a one-night stand after a romantic dinner for two.

He shook his head, wondering how it would be to unlace her a little, though. Make her purr and smile as he knew his hands on her warm, curving body could do. A jolt of desire made him grip the cold handle of his shopping cart hard.

'Can I help you, sir?' an aproned clerk broke in on his lusty thoughts.

'Not unless you have an antidote for aphrodisia,' he said.

The clerk blinked, opened her mouth and gave him a startled look.

'Just kidding,' he said.

Then he rumbled his cart away.

★   ★   ★

Instead of finding Jenny in the lobby with her nephew, he saw Grace Douglas next to the circular desk, leaning on it with one elbow and talking to the male receptionist. She looked up from her conversation and gave Parker the once-over.

'Well, there he is, our seller of *Pseudotsuga taxifolia* and *Picea pungens*.'

Parker blinked. His Latin was sketchy, but he did recognize the scientific names for his Douglas fir and blue spruce.

'Uh, right,' he replied.

138

'The one who carries on our grand tradition of Yule-tide,' Grace continued.

Parker knit his brows, interpreting her hyperbole to refer to his job selling greenery at Christmas time.

'I guess you could say that.'

She led him through the lobby to the carpeted parlor area, where their tree stood proudly garbed in colorful decorations, with a bright gold star on top. Light bouncing in from the window caught the star and made it gleam. It was one of his best trees, he agreed.

'As long as people enjoy it, then it makes me feel good,' he said.

Grace dropped her theatrical speech and leaned closer, as if to share a special thought.

'I happen to be in the market for some greenery myself,' she intoned. 'I wondered if you might have something to show me.'

Parker struggled for an appropriate response. Inwardly, he could not help but be amused by her innuendos. Clearly, this woman was angling for a date. How could he refuse politely without wounding her ego?

'I, um, think you'd find a tree to your liking on my lot,' he said. 'I'm going there as soon as I pick up Roger West. He's agreed to help me out today.'

'Ah, yes, the young sprout. Rather big of you to take the young man under your wing. I do admire a man who loves children.'

'Well, that's not too hard.'

'Oh, I think that to some people who haven't been exposed to children, it is a near miracle. To see into the working minds of young creatures can be unfathomable to the uninitiated.'

'I wouldn't go that far.'

'I, on the other hand, might go much farther.'

Her expressive voice left no doubt as to what she would like to go farther with, and he cleared his throat, running a hand around the back of his neck. He felt suddenly awkward.

He scanned the lobby and consulted his watch, trying to send a signal that he needed to get going.

'Young Roger's temporary guardian asked me to take charge of him until you arrived,' said Grace. 'She had an errand to complete.'

In spite of Parker's resolve that Jenny Knight was not for him, he could not help the disappointment that crept into his reply.

'I see.'

'You'll find the lad dispensing balls across the green felt with the tip of a hard cue.'

Parker blinked. 'You mean on the pool table in the rec room?'

'Exactly.'

'Thanks.'

He took the stairs to the lower level and followed the sound of knocking wooden balls to the rec room. A pool table sat to one side of a nondescript room with stationary bicycles at the other end. Folding card tables rested against the wall. He waited until Roger finished his shot.

'Hello, young man.'

'Hullo.'

'Are you ready to go sell some Christmas trees?'

'Yeah, sure.' He put his cue away. 'You got a CD player in your truck?'

'No, but we can listen to 'Mostly Mozart' on National Public Radio if you like.'

He couldn't resist teasing the boy. Like his aunt, Roger West took himself and his own culture too seriously. Parker couldn't resist the urge to see what he could do to broaden the boy's horizon. But only with good humor.

But Roger was quick. Hands on hips, he aimed his brown-eyed stare at Parker. 'What were Bach's dates?'

Startled, Parker frowned. 'Well, let's see, 17 — no, 16 — ' He shook his head. 'I don't know. You got me there. What were his dates?'

'Mostly with Mrs. Bach,' replied Roger.

Then he laughed boisterously while Parker shook his head, handing him his coat.

'Touché,' he said.

Grace still stood at the desk when they climbed the stairs back to the lobby. He hoped to glide past her without being waylaid this time, but the persistent woman stopped him, inspecting Roger's clothes to make sure he would be warm enough. Jenny's instructions? Parker wondered.

'You will be giving the girls and boys a break from the cold, I trust?' Grace queried him.

'Sure. There's a trailer where they can take breaks. And it's a sunny day. Though they say snow is coming in tonight.'

'Speaking of warming up,' said Grace, 'I hope you'll join us for a cup of hot cider when you return.'

Parker remained noncommittal. 'Well, I don't know. I'll work late after I drop the kids off.'

'About those directions to your lot . . . ' she reminded him. 'Mustn't forget my tree.'

He obligingly wrote directions to the lot on a piece of paper at the desk, tore it off and handed it to her. She pressed the directions to her chest.

'I look forward to our encounter,' she intoned.

Perplexed, Parker gave her a nod and scooted Roger out to the truck. He'd dawdled too long already. His partner, Gary, had recuperated enough to be at the lot this morning, but his doctors had told him not to work. He was to rest in the trailer and let the boys do the hard work.

'Let's go, young man,' Parker said to his newest recruit. 'Time to earn that football.'

* * *

Jenny emerged from the corridor at the far end of the parlor area just as Parker ripped off the piece of paper and handed it to Grace. She saw her program director bat her eyelashes at Parker and clutch the paper to her breast.

Whoa! thought Jenny. What was going on here? Parker and Grace again. What was that man up to? She'd been so bowled over by his sincere emotions last night and his suave ease this morning that she had begun to weaken. Now what was he doing?

It angered Jenny, and she steeled her heart to her earlier feelings. Parker McAllister was a man of many faces, showing off whichever one might be most useful at the moment. Comfortable anywhere, was he? She became indignant at the thought of his behavior, and irritated with Grace. But if Jenny tried to offer any more advice on the subject, it would look as if she was trying to get Parker for herself.

She waited until Parker had left and then approached the front desk stiffly, intent upon reaching her office. But Grace hailed her.

'I have seen your young charge safely into the hands of his protector.'

Jenny couldn't help but try to peek at what Parker had written on the paper in Grace's hand. But she folded it into a small square and tucked it into the opening of her shirt. Jenny's mouth dropped open.

'Good heavens, Grace. Don't you have any pockets?'

Grace gave her a look that conveyed great confidentiality and intrigue.

'Some items are too important for mere pockets.'

Jenny shut her eyes. The woman was really going too far. It was on the tip of her tongue to ask her just exactly what was too dear for her pockets that must instead be secured in her bosom. But she could not bring herself to pry, at least not in front of the watchful eye of the desk attendant.

'I'll be in my office,' she told them both and stalked off.

However, the mystery was solved a moment later, when Grace followed her into the office.

'I have obtained directions to Parker McAllister's Christmas tree lot,' she said. 'I

144

have decided to buy a Christmas tree.'

Jenny looked at her program director as if the woman had lost her mind. 'We have a tree.'

'Not for here,' said Grace, waving an arm. 'For my own apartment. I thought some Christmas cheer would not be misplaced.'

Jenny leaned her elbows on her desk. 'How noble of you.'

She turned her head to gaze out her window, which gave a view of the front lawn, sloping beside the drive up to the street. The trees were swaying hard as wind beat against the eaves. A front was moving in, that was for sure.

'I suppose I might have to get a tree for Roger. I have a funny feeling his parents won't be back until Christmas, if then. The kid ought to have a tree, I suppose.'

'Splendid. Then let us go forth and choose our greenery.'

Jenny leaned back, tilting her chair with her weight. 'Can't you go and pick one out for me?'

Grace placed a hand on her chest. 'Never. I might make the wrong selection. Only you know what height and breadth will fit in your abode. Come now. You can't do inventory all day long. It's Christmas.'

Jenny pushed a hand through her hair. 'It's

also the month the corporate office is going to send a team to inspect. I can't let anything drop. I have to work for at least a few hours today.'

'Agreed. You can work for three hours, no longer. We should make tree selections before it gets too late.'

Reluctantly, Jenny agreed. 'I suppose you're right there. It *is* supposed to snow this evening.'

Grace left her at last, and Jenny spent the next several hours running accounts. With her tightening up everything at the home, their finances were showing definite improvement. The numbers eeked upward. She just needed to check a few more details before she could finalize things for the coming inspection. She prayed nobody quit this week, or next.

'Please just get us through December,' she said to herself.

By the time her computer screen made her eyes blur, she was ready for a break. Lured out by Grace into the windy afternoon, Jenny rode grumpily in the car. While Grace exclaimed over the many Christmas decorations along the way, all Jenny could think about was that she'd rather they were buying trees from a different lot. But she considered that her presence was needed on two counts: Grace might be tempted to buy additional

146

greenery for their grand Christmas production, which their budget couldn't afford, and she needed to make sure Roger wasn't causing Parker too much trouble. She still felt irritated at Grace's dramatics over Parker, though inside a secret place, she was glad Parker hadn't been giving Grace his phone number.

The thought that she ought to see about doing something with Roger that evening also niggled at her. She admitted to herself that it might be fun to make some popcorn and watch a movie with her nephew tonight. As long as she finished her paperwork by dinner time, of course. She would have to make sure they didn't dally at the lot. She tried to hold on to her feelings of resentment, using them as added weight to her irritation that Christmas existed at all.

She sat with her arms folded across her chest, still frowning out the window at the upscale shops in Cherry Creek. Gazing at the beautifully decorated windows only reminded her of the elaborate Christmas she'd had with Drake last year. The shopping, the gifts, the champagne evenings. It still hurt Jenny to remember the words and promises spoken over candlelit dinners, the warm and fuzzy dream of security she'd begun to nourish. Then, nine months later, he had told her that he had a greater dream than the one he was sharing with her. The glow had worn off. Drake hadn't been in it for the long haul. She hadn't been his future; she'd only been a convenience for him.

She shut her eyes from the humiliation of it. She'd thought she'd been in love. Looking back now, she suspected that she'd only been in love with the comfort of a handsome date. With his ability to show her a good time. Perhaps her pride had been damaged more than her heart had been broken. She opened her eyes again.

But she insisted on hanging on to her martyr status. Remembering these thoughts helped her make sure she didn't get involved again. Today she would consider herself a chaperone for Grace, who might not be able to control her lusty interest in Parker McAllister.

'It's snowing,' cried Grace. 'What a lovely sight.'

The flakes were beginning to powder the windshield. Light flakes that didn't look like much yet. But the iron-gray clouds that darkened the sky overhead warned of more to come.

'It's a good thing we're here now,' said Grace. 'Wouldn't want to get stuck out here if it's going to get bad.'

'Then we won't stay long at the lot,' said Jenny.

Grace turned to study her boss silently at a long red light. 'You really don't like our tree expert, do you?'

'I just don't like what he represents.'

'Which is?'

Jenny exhaled slowly. 'A dashing bachelor ready to sweep a willing woman off her feet. He shouldn't be trusted.'

'Sweeping judgment, isn't it? You don't even know the man.'

'That's just the point.'

'I'm not sure I follow the point,' said Grace. The light turned green.

'What I'm trying to say is that a man like that can be deceptive. Looks aren't everything. You'd better be careful of your own vulnerability, Grace. I'd hate to see you hurt by him.'

'Well, the fun is in the chase, so they say. But I think you do him a disservice.'

'How so?'

'Well, that's for you to decide.' Grace's voice lost none of its lilt. 'I just think you aren't giving him a chance.'

'And I don't plan to.'

'Suit yourself.'

They ended the discussion by slowing down in the residential area of Cherry Creek

North, mostly built up with new town homes. Just a few of the older red-brick bungalows remained. Mature elms and maples gave the neighborhood a graceful feel, and Jenny couldn't help but be impressed with the size and quality of Parker's lot.

Grace squeezed into a parking space by the curb, lined bumper-to-bumper with residents and Parker's customers. And a busy lot it was. Two teenagers were tying a tree onto the roof of a Toyota. Jenny heard Roger's voice before she saw him.

'Those are eight-foot trees. Ten-footers are over here.'

She and Grace came around the string fence to the main avenue, where Roger was leading a middle-aged couple down the row. Parker broke off from talking to one of the teenage boys when he saw them and nearly collided with a woman and her dog, crossing an intersection in the rows of trees. Jenny inhaled the scent of greenery and followed Grace into the lot.

Parker's eyes found Jenny's immediately, and she turned, pretending interest in some small potted trees, while Grace complimented Parker on the assemblage. She went on to explain her needs, while Jenny fingered the silky, pointed pine needles.

'Perhaps Roger can show you some trees,'

suggested Parker. 'He's become very adept at helping folks.'

'Splendid,' said Grace. And she marched off to examine the merchandise.

The gaiety of people selecting trees was almost infectious, but Jenny lowered her eyes when Parker came over. He was bundled up in a green parka with a red lining, and his cheeks were ruddy from being out in the fresh, cold air all day.

'Hello,' he said.

'Hello.' The sting of attraction still enveloped them, as much as she wanted to deny it.

'Are you shopping for a tree?' he asked.

Her heart danced inside her. She felt as if he'd asked her whether she was shopping for a man, not a tree. She glanced out from under her eyelashes.

'No . . . well, yes. That is, since Roger may be here right up until Christmas, I thought maybe I should decorate.'

Parker's face relaxed into pleasure. 'Good idea. You came to the right place, then.'

'Hmmm.'

'How big a tree do you want?'

She shrugged, hugging her arms to herself. 'Not too big. You've seen my apartment,' she said self-consciously. 'I can put it next to the fireplace, I think.'

He touched her elbow to guide her away from the small potted trees and toward something larger.

'These firs last several weeks.'

He dropped her elbow to shake a tree loose from those it stood next to. It was full and green and perfect. She did feel a small nip at her heart, as if the tree was just begging to be taken home and cared for.

'That one is fine,' she said. Then she realized what she'd done wrong and blushed in her embarrassment.

Her eyes widened as she looked at Parker. 'I haven't brought my car. I came with Grace.'

But Parker half-smiled to himself as he fussed with the tree. 'No problem. I'll bring it in the pickup when I drop Roger back.'

Right, thought Jenny. He does have to bring Roger home.

'Thanks. I guess I just wasn't thinking.'

His eyes found hers. 'I'm sure you were thinking too hard, in fact. Roger told me you were working today.'

The way he said it made her knees shake.

'Well, yes, I was. I'm afraid Grace dragged me out.'

'I'll have to thank her for it.'

Zing went that uncontrollable feeling of intimacy he managed to conjure up. Just practiced charm, she tried to tell herself.

Parker hoisted the tree to his shoulder and carried it down the row toward a trailer that had a big banner with the words CHRISTMAS TREES in tall, red capital letters on the front. He carried her tree around the corner and set it down. Then he brushed off his hands and came back to where she'd followed him.

She came to her senses as he returned. 'How much do I owe you?'

He grinned. 'Let's step into my office and settle up.'

He reached up to the trailer door and opened it, motioning her toward the two steps leading inside. She was curious about his setup, and she realized she hadn't seen Sydney anywhere. Perhaps the girl was inside, warming up. So Jenny took the steps and entered the trailer. Parker followed her, and the door swung shut.

It was a neat place. A metal desk sat under the window where one could watch the lot. On the other side of the door was a brown plaid couch, and beyond that a small kitchen area. Perhaps Sydney was resting in the back. A narrow door seemed to lead to another room. But no little girl's voice called out to them.

'This is nice,' she said, just to have something to say.

Parker moved around her to the desk and leaned over to pick up a receipt book. He seemed to fill the small room with his masculine size and bearing. He scribbled out the price of the tree and then stood to hand it to her.

She realized she was staring at him stupidly and wished she would get over the way he affected her. Now, why had she come in here with him? Couldn't she have waited outside while he got the receipt?

He was looking at her silently, his eyes conveying private thoughts of his own. Then the inevitable happened again. He moved closer, still holding the receipt in his hand. He didn't even touch her, just looked at her as the electricity crackled between them.

Finally, she looked down, reaching for the receipt, but when she touched it, his other hand closed over hers.

'Jenny,' he said, in that deep, melodic voice that plucked at her heartstrings, no matter how hard she tried to resist. 'I'm glad you came.'

She wasn't looking at his face, and she swallowed hard. Damn! This wasn't going to work. Was she so desperate that she had followed him in here to tempt fate?

'I — ' she tried, but no words came out.

Instead, her body began to tingle as his

empty hand came up to brush her face. His chilly fingers played with the hair that sprang out from under her white wool cap. Why didn't she move away? Why did she just stand there like a dolt? She knew the answer, even though she didn't want to admit it to herself.

From outside, the voices of customers and kids mingled in the bustle of holiday shopping. A background to the tingling excitement within the trailer. She suddenly wanted Parker to sweep her into his arms and kiss her. She wanted to find out what he'd almost offered last night, standing on the deck. Could she have been wrong to be so suspicious of him? Perhaps what was resonating between them was real. Perhaps the only way to find out was to lower her guard and test the waters.

The bells were ringing in her head, and when he slowly drew her closer, she didn't resist. The bulk of their clothing lay between them, but it didn't matter. His warm lips found hers, and she parted hers in startled wonder. His kiss was tentative at first, and then stronger. She heard the receipt crinkle as he clasped both arms around her. Her own arms reached around him and she opened her lips farther, drinking in the kiss.

Oh, my, she sighed. *I've forgotten what this was like.* And it was like no other kiss she could remember in her entire life. For a moment she forgot caution and simply enjoyed it. A deepening kiss from a man who desired her. The chemistry between them made her heart race, and she felt the warm inner glow that came with it. Joy leapt upward and she kissed him back. So what if there was no tomorrow? People needed kissing, and she was going to indulge in a reckless moment.

He held her tighter, until the drumming in her head threatened to burst. Then he let go of her lips and brushed her ear with his mouth. She gasped for breath, clinging to him. Finally, gently, he let her go. But he kissed her forehead then, smiling down at her.

'Thank you,' he said with a teasing smile on his face. 'I needed that.'

Jenny just stared at him, thinking she might fall down if his hand didn't still support her. She blinked and tried to gather her wits about her.

'I — ' she choked out.

Parker's grin widened. 'I think you said that before.'

She tried to dredge up some of her usual flare. 'I don't usually do that,' was all she could think of to say.

Her lips were still throbbing and she looked

at the desk, rather than have to meet his gaze. But he wasn't through with her yet. His hand brushed her cheek, tucking her hair back.

'Jenny,' he said in a more serious voice, 'I'd better get back outside. But I was wondering . . .'

'Uh, what?'

'I was wondering if I could see you tonight.'

She swallowed. Yes, her body wanted to scream; she wanted more of what he'd just done to her. But how? And how fast did she want to go? Surely not . . . She stopped her thoughts before they could wander too far.

She shrugged. 'I'll see you when you bring the tree and Roger home.'

'Yeah,' he said. He smoothed out the crumpled receipt and handed it to her again. 'Does that mean you're giving me an invitation?'

She dug in her purse for the money. She was forced to meet his gleaming dark eyes as she handed the bills to him.

'Well,' she said cautiously, 'I promised Roger I'd make hamburgers. You can join us if you like.'

He took the bills and slowly unzipped his money belt. His eyes traveled over her face, making every nerve in her body tingle again. She read some caution in his eyes now, some hesitancy that had replaced the spontaneous burning passion of a moment ago. He must be struggling with what was happening between them, too. Well, that was good, Jenny rationalized. Maybe he would want to go slow.

'I'd like that,' he said, nodding, almost as if to himself. 'I'd like that just fine.'

7

Jenny followed him outside, hoping the cold and the light, moist flakes drifting down to dampen her nose and cheeks would bring her back to her senses. The lot was in a flurry of activity as the boys helped customers haul trees to their vehicles. She heard Grace picking out a tree and talking to the others as Roger and one of the teenage boys laid a blanket on the top of her car and tied the tree onto her ski rack.

Parker moved about the lot, making sure the customers got what they wanted. All the while she stood about absently, thinking about the kiss. Was this what she wanted? Her inner trembling said yes. Her mind warned her with a no.

She was being weak-willed and at the moment was losing the battle with herself. She couldn't help her thrill of excitement and pleasure at the sight of Parker's dark, uncovered head, just barely brushed with some of the small snowflakes. The snow wasn't heavy yet, but they'd better finish their business here and get home before it started to make driving difficult.

Commanding her feet to move, Jenny walked slowly to the car. She still had enough wits about her to stop and get Roger's attention. After all, she had a job to do here. She was a chaperone for her nephew, and she mustn't ignore that responsibility. At the moment, her nephew was darting around the lot with more energy than he'd ever shown in her presence. Another indicator that Parker had been right. He'd offered the boy something productive he wanted to do. Well, some people had a way with children. Parker must be one of them.

It wasn't until she and Grace were snug in the car that she remembered to feel guilty. Grace was the one with the obvious interest in Parker. Was Jenny being disloyal, inviting Parker to dinner? She'd never really believed Parker and Grace would be right for each other, and now she tried to remember all the reasons she had been so determined to warn Grace about him. And here she was falling victim to his lure herself. What should she say?

Grace didn't seem bothered by the fact that Parker and Jenny had spent a great deal of time together in the trailer. Perhaps no one else had noticed. But Grace carried on with her usual enthusiasm about the trees, the snow and the holiday decorations.

'Grace,' Jenny finally interrupted, her own emotions in turmoil, 'how can you be so excited about everything all the time?'

The question struck Grace dumb. She glanced, open-mouthed, at Jenny as they waited for a light to change. Her silence was so lengthy, Jenny started to feel bad that she'd stunned the woman to silence and started to amend her words.

'I mean, it's good that you're so upbeat. I guess I admire it, that's all. I can't seem to muster so much enthusiasm myself.'

She hoped that explained her invasive question.

Grace grinned and put her foot on the gas. 'I guess it's a habit that comes from the way I do my job. You put a smile on, and pretty soon everyone around you is smiling too.'

'Yes,' Jenny agreed. 'You're right. I guess I haven't found much to smile about lately.'

She glanced sideways at Grace's profile. 'I guess it's just not in my nature.'

'You've had a lot on your shoulders,' Grace said. 'Trying to save the place and all. We all know how hard you've worked to make our numbers look good for corporate. With that success behind you, you'll have something to smile about, won't you?'

'Well, yes,' said Jenny, frowning.

Talking about her responsibilities at work

161

helped take her mind off the dangerous temptation offered by Parker McAllister. She sighed. It also reminded her of how much work there was left to be done. But she still wanted to be honest with Grace about Parker.

'Uh, Grace, Parker is going to stop over to my place for a hamburger tonight, when he delivers my tree.' She felt a flush of embarrassment.

'Oh?'

Damn! This was awkward. What was she thinking of, anyway? Suddenly, a way out presented itself, and she spoke the words that came first into her head.

'Perhaps you'd like to join us, Roger and Parker and me.'

There was barely a pause as Grace considered. 'Splendid. Tasty hamburgers while our dashing hero sets up your tree.'

'I hope you don't mind.'

'Mind?'

'Um, that he's bringing my tree, I mean.'

Two heartbeats of a pause. 'Well, why should I?'

Jenny shoved her elbow on the armrest and folded her fingers under the chin. She stared out the window, trying to think of a way to explain what was going on. Finally, she decided the truth was best. Grace always confronted things head-on. Maybe she should do the same. She turned to look at her co-worker again.

'I know you're interested in him, Grace. And he is supposed to be off-limits for me. It was my fault that I invited him to stay for dinner after he brings the tree. I don't want things to get, uh, complicated.'

Her cheeks flamed, but she carried on. 'I don't want it to look like I'm trying to . . . to . . . '

Grace chuckled. 'To snatch him out from under me?'

'Right.'

Grace's chuckle turned into good-humored laughter as she guided the car carefully into traffic.

'Fair is fair. I haven't managed to get him under me, have I, now? So any snatching is simply determined by who gets him first.'

'Grace!'

Jenny's emotions still stirred with guilt and confusion. Grace's willingness to turn it all into a game only shocked her further.

Grace was smiling to herself in amusement. 'If it is you he prefers, that is not a problem. I just thought such a delicious, eligible morsel should not go to waste.'

Jenny blinked at Grace's imagery, swallowing hard. But Grace's metaphor served as a wake-up call. She needed to pull back before she crossed the line that had been so clearly drawn. She couldn't risk Parker coming to her apartment for the evening alone. Only if Grace turned up too would it prevent the gossips' tongues from wagging.

'Then you'll come?' asked Jenny.

'To eat hamburgers and decorate your tree? Of course. It sounds like a delightful thing to do.'

⋆   ⋆   ⋆

Several hours later, Parker loaded Jenny's tree into the truck and then opened the door for Sydney to climb up. His partner, Gary, drove up and rolled down his window.

The forty-five-year-old man smiled at him. 'How's it going?'

Parker came over to fill Gary in on the progress of the day. 'Great. We had a busy day. I've got the night deposit. Will you and the boys be okay tonight?'

'Shouldn't be a problem,' said Gary. Parker noted that his color was good, and he was heartened by the man's recovery since his heart attack.

'Just don't work too hard,' Parker cautioned him. 'Let those boys of yours haul the trees.'

'Don't worry.' Gary grinned. 'That's what I pay them to do.'

The other man waved at Sydney and then drove his car on into the lot to park it beside the trailer.

With everything taken care of, Parker only had to make the night deposit at the bank and then stop at home to clean up. Roger squeezed into the narrow jumpseat in the truck behind Sydney and Parker.

'You tired, chicken?' he asked Sydney, who leaned quietly against the seat.

'Yes,' she answered.

He ruffled her hair. 'You had a long day. Well, how about a hot bath and then something to eat?'

'Ummm-hmmm.'

Parker's muscles were tired, but he knew a hot shower would revive him. A pleasant evening stretched ahead, the kind he hadn't anticipated in a long time. Jenny hadn't exactly invited Sydney for hamburgers, but surely she realized he had his daughter for the weekend. Thinking of Jenny and the way she'd responded to his kiss made heat spiral inside him. Of course they couldn't do anything with the kids present. And he wondered just how far Jenny would want to go.

But sex wasn't the only issue here. These

days sex meant responsibility, and both he and Jenny had a lot of that on their shoulders. He wondered at the wisdom of following where their instincts were leading them. Sex alone wouldn't be enough, and he wasn't sure he was ready for the rest. He'd relied on the boundaries she had wordlessly drawn when they'd met. Now he wondered what he would do if she tore those boundaries down.

★   ★   ★

By the time Parker arrived with the tree, Jenny had a place for it beside the brick fireplace. Grace bustled around the kitchen, washing lettuce and chopping onions. Jenny supervised Roger at setting the table. If she worried about it becoming a romantic evening, it was a far cry from it. And she felt grateful that she wasn't spending Saturday evening alone.

It made her feel good that she had friends here, and even her nephew to help make her feel she wasn't alone. She had dreaded the Christmas season because it reminded her of the beginning of a relationship last year that had gone nowhere. She didn't want to get trapped into anything similar. But she realized she couldn't shut herself off from

166

people either. Decorating her tree with this rambunctious group was a good thing. A piece of her stone heart chipped away. Maybe she could enjoy the season just a little bit, as long as she kept everything in perspective.

But when she opened the door to see Parker, his dark hair still damp from his shower, loose charcoal crewneck sweater draping his muscular shoulders, her heart did that dance that was becoming so familiar.

'Come in.' She pushed the door wider.

He paused to glance across the living room toward the activity in the kitchen, where Grace and Roger were clanging around. His crooked grin relaxed her nervousness.

'I left Sydney at Mom's,' he said. 'She was so tired, she decided she'd rather sleep than eat.'

He looked at her a little apologetically as he picked up the tree to carry it in. And Jenny understood his meaning. He would have to include Sydney in all his weekend plans. So much the better. Being responsible for the kids would keep them from indulging their humming glands. After that kiss today, it was all too obvious what was going on between them. The group gathering would help her keep her wits about her.

Parker set the tree in the stand, then brushed off his hands. He greeted the others and then exclaimed over the hamburgers piled high on a platter. After all the food was on the table, they sat down to dig in.

Between grunts of satisfaction and swipes of napkins to wipe mustard and catsup off lips, they all chattered about the events of the day. Roger was quite proud of having earned his football and said he would work again next Saturday if he could earn something else.

Parker exchanged a knowing look with Jenny. 'No problem, son. I know you'll enjoy what you've earned yourself.'

They stuffed themselves to bursting and then all helped clean up. After which, they lit into a box of Christmas decorations Jenny had saved from last year. She thought it might be painful to handle the decorations she and Drake had purchased together, but she found that the sting was gone. They were only tinsel and glitter, after all. It was the joy and warmth of sharing them with others that gave them meaning.

They laughed and argued about the placement of carved wooden reindeer, cuckoo clocks and bears, and then Parker produced a special package that he made Jenny unwrap. She trembled as she tore away the red paper and held up a beautiful silver, glitter-covered star.

'It's lovely,' she said. 'Does it go on the top?'

Parker nodded from where he sat on the floor, an arm draped over one bent knee drawn close to his body.

'It does.'

Grace watched them for a moment and then roused Roger, who was lying under the tree, looking up through its branches.

'Roger, my laddie, why don't you help me put these things away and then show me that computer game.'

'Can't,' Roger uttered from beneath the tree.

'Why not?' asked Grace.

'Aunt Jenny's computer is off-limits.'

Grace raised an eyebrow. 'Oh, I see. Well, young man, I have a sterling idea. How would you like to come to my house and play computer games?'

Grace smiled at Jenny, though she still spoke to Roger. 'Computer games are my weakness.'

Jenny's eyes widened. She didn't know Grace indulged in computer games, but she did know what the other woman was doing. She opened her mouth to object that she shouldn't go so soon, but Grace's penetrating look told her that she knew very well what she was doing. The exuberant program director's words came back to her: 'Such a delicious, eligible morsel as Parker McAllister should not go to waste.' Evidently, she had read the signals that were passing between Jenny and Parker and decided to retreat gracefully.

That thought made Jenny flush nervously. She hastened to be the gracious hostess even as a hot fear flashed through her. She wasn't sure she was prepared to be left alone with Parker. The only blessing might be a chance to talk to him, to clarify what was happening.

She cleared her throat and got to her feet. 'Grace, are you sure you want to go? I hate to see you have to drive back here later.'

'Ah, yes, but the young sprout needs to exercise his mind.'

'He does?' Jenny asked vaguely.

'Of course,' replied Grace. 'After a day of invigorating work and a hearty meal, he must put his brain to work in order to round out his day. Besides' — she winked — 'I haven't had a chance to dive into WarCraft since I bought it. The shrinkwrap is still intact.'

'Well, if you think . . . ' Jenny's protests were swept away by Roger, coming to life again.

'WarCraft? Wow! Orcs versus humans. Can I be a human?'

Grace eyed him critically. 'We'll have to read what the specifications are for humans.'

Then they were all on their feet. Coats were retrieved and hasty good evenings exchanged. At the door, Grace gave Jenny another wink.

'I'll have the lad back by ten o'clock. Will that be sufficient? For bedtime, I mean. We have to make sure he gets eight hours of shut-eye.'

Jenny flushed. She knew very well what Grace was alluding to, and she was suddenly terrified. She swallowed. 'Sure, fine. See you at ten.'

After closing the door, she turned to face Parker, unable to meet his eyes.

'Um, would you like some decaf coffee?'

'Hmmm, sounds good. Can I help?'

It might help if he stood on the opposite side of the counter that separated the kitchen from the dining area, she thought. Already she felt nervous trembling seize her as she walked to the kitchen. But he didn't stay on the other side of the counter. He followed her into the kitchen and sat on a stool, stretching one arm across the counter.

She poured milk into a ceramic creamer and shoved it and the sugar bowl along the counter toward him. She was aware that his eyes followed her, and she could hardly stifle the throb that sprang between them. My God, this man didn't even have to touch her

171

to make her body pulse with the rhythm of desire. How was she going to fend off the inevitable?

After she got the coffee brewing in the coffeemaker, she turned to face him, her arms crossed as she leaned against the counter.

'We should talk,' she croaked.

'Hmmm,' he said, passion suffusing his face.

When he got up to move toward her, she fought a losing battle. His arms went around her waist and his face lowered to within inches of hers.

'Somehow talking wasn't what I thought this was all about.'

Parker knew better than to do what he was about to do. But Jenny Knight had gotten far deeper under his skin than he wanted to admit. She was in a place now where his impulses were going to take over from his rational plans. When that door had shut, leaving them alone, he took it as a sign from her that it was okay if he kissed her again. He had waited patiently while she made the coffee, feasting his eyes on her luscious body in her ribbed cotton sweater and jeans that showed off round hips and firm buttocks. All evening his hands had itched to hold her again.

And now she was in his arms. But she was

fighting what was between them as much as he had at first.

'I want you, Jenny,' he whispered. 'You make me want to do foolish things with you.'

For an answer, she gurgled something half protest, half passion. But he didn't want to force himself on her. It was just pure chemistry between them. Maybe they should slow down.

But when he parted her lips with his tongue and felt her arms snake around him, lust crashed through his veins. It almost seemed like forbidden fruit, holding a soft, curving woman close against him for a few hours away from other responsibilities. *Escape with me, Jenny*, he wanted to say to her. *Let's forget the problems of the world and take this gift of pleasure.*

When she moaned softly against him, he knew he was lost. His hands and hers stroked and felt, exploring each other hungrily. He kissed her cheek, working his way to her throat as she threw her head back, letting her mane of hair fall over his hands. Her sweater was up high enough that he could seek the comfort of her breasts, and he knew with certainty that he wouldn't be satisfied until he had all of her.

'Is this what you want?' he asked hoarsely, as his fingers worked to unleash her breasts.

173

'Parker,' she moaned. 'I, we . . . shouldn't.'

'I won't if you don't want me to,' he murmured.

Still, he nuzzled her neck and grasped her buttocks to press her against his bulging, aching desire. Somehow he got her onto the stool, still warm from when he'd rested there. Her legs locked around him and she drank him in.

'I'll stop,' he said crazily. But how?

'Just kiss me, Jenny,' he begged.

And kiss him she did. Her arms wrapped around his neck, and her fingers dug through his hair as her mouth trembled against his and their tongues entangled. She must not have been loved in a long time, her trembling was that of someone long deprived. And he had been deprived as well, more than he'd realized.

He wanted to carry her to the bedroom. They had the time. They might not soon get it again.

'Jenny?' he asked, hoping she would read his mind.

'Parker, I . . . ' she croaked out.

He felt the slightest pressure of her hands against his shoulders and pulled away. He would have to do something about the pulsing, aching throb of blood in his lower regions, but he tried to ignore his pain.

'What?' he asked softly, planting a kiss on her ear. 'What do you want me to do?'

'It's not what I want you to do,' she finally said breathlessly. 'It's what I can't afford to do.'

That penetrated. 'What do you mean?'

She let her hand slide down his sweater. 'It's against the rules.'

'What rules?'

She shook her head and managed to pull herself back, leaning against the counter.

'You're the relative of one of my . . . residents.'

He eased off, regretfully. 'Ohhh, I see. Off-limits?'

She nodded, her cheeks still pink with passion.

He let his hands rest on the counter behind her, still so close that they could hear each other's breathing.

'I don't want to do anything that would cause you to lose your job.'

He had meant it as a joke, but she nodded seriously, brushing some of her hair back from her face.

'The spy would turn me in.'

He blinked. 'The spy?'

She eased off the stool and moved away from him, leaving him feeling bereft. He saw how unsteady her hands were when she poured the coffee.

'Someone in the home is spying on me.'

He leaned against the counter, trying to get himself in a more comfortable position, and crossed his arms.

'What are you talking about?'

She handed him a mug. 'I know someone is spying on me because corporate headquarters hears about things that go on here before I have a chance to turn in my reports.'

He stirred in some milk and then sipped the hot coffee, taking what comfort he could from it.

'Are you serious?'

'Yes.'

She poured milk into her own coffee and then climbed up on the other stool. She still looked incredibly sexy, and he still wanted to sweet-talk her into the bedroom. But he also wanted to hear what she had to say. He knew suddenly deep down that he wanted to hear everything she had to say about anything.

So he disciplined his mind to just listening and looking. Wondering what made her so uptight about her job since he had seen her passion and knew she wasn't really laced up so tight. But some of the tension was back in her bearing now, and he wanted to know what made her so tense. Her job? He'd had a job like that once and had learned how to let go of it. Maybe Jenny needed to ease up on the stress in her life.

One step at a time, old boy, he told himself. He hadn't wanted to get trapped again in a relationship with a woman who wanted to control everything. But it was hard to hear the warning bells when his glands were driving him. He let his eyes drift back to her face and met her smoky gaze.

'Well, then, tell me about your spy.'

She pulled her mouth to the side exasperatedly. 'I don't know who it is. I can't figure it out.'

'What sort of things are reported?'

She shook her head, stirring her coffee some more. 'When the help quits. When the electricity goes out. Even when our little bus needed a new carburetor.'

Parker stared at her. 'You think someone knows I'm here with you now?'

She tilted her head and sipped the coffee. 'Possibly. I shouldn't have let Grace and Roger go.'

Parker's lips quirked into an amused grin as he glanced toward the French doors that led to her balcony. He remembered that that side of the building faced open space. If Jenny's spy was inside the retirement home, surely he wouldn't be watching there.

'Well,' he said, 'I don't want to get you in trouble.'

Defiance swept over Jenny's face for a brief moment. 'I know it's silly. But I have to put up with it at least for another few weeks.'

'What happens in another few weeks?'

'Corporate is sending a team here. It's an annual procedure. But everything has to be perfect. They'll do an inspection and evaluation.'

She wasn't looking at him now. Her hands pulled her hair back from her face and she puffed air into her cheeks and let it out. While she still might be trying to come down from their passion, he suspected there was more to this than she wanted to say. But he wouldn't push her. She'd tell him what was on her mind in her own good time.

He chuckled. 'I once had a job similar to yours. Oh, not at a retirement home, certainly. But marketing electronics was stressful. I realize that now.'

She looked at him with curiosity in her eyes. 'They let you go.'

'That's right.'

'And you haven't made up your mind about what to do next.'

'Nope,' he said. 'But I'm not worried about it. Something will come up.'

She wrinkled a brow at that. 'I always

thought you have to make things happen.'

'Well,' he drawled, 'you have to have faith that things will work out. Sometimes you just can't force things.'

He tried to read the troubled expression in her eyes and wanted to comfort her. He wanted her to unburden her troubles on his shoulder, but at the same time he understood the need for professional discretion. She did run the place his mother lived in. It wasn't any of his business how she did her job, as long as he made sure his mother was well taken care of. In fact, in some quirky way, he could see how Jenny worried that the spy, if there really was one, might think he was trying to get inside information.

He shook his head. Now he was getting as carried away as Jenny. He drained the coffee and set down the mug. He let his eyes roam over her tousled hair and inflamed face. He still fought the temptation of what he wanted to do, but all the barriers were still in place. And most ironic of all, even should he throw caution to the wind and pretend there was no tomorrow, a spy might report them!

'Guess I'd better be getting Sydney home,' he muttered.

She nodded regretfully. 'It must be a lot for you, caring for your daughter on the weekends and . . . and managing a business.'

He sensed her feeling of awkwardness and wasn't sure whether he should be flattered or alarmed that she was poking around in his personal affairs. That was the problem; neither of them wanted anyone else poking into what was private. And he realized the dangers of falling for someone you wanted to change. You couldn't change a person. You were who you were until *you* wanted to change.

It helped him cool off his desire. If he made love to a woman at this stage of the game, it had to be for keeps. And he didn't have the kind of life in place where he could play for keeps.

She followed him to the door. 'Didn't you wear a coat? The snow must be coming down harder now.'

'Left it at Mom's. Just a dash across the parking lot.'

Her eyes still looked dreamy, and she tilted her face up in a very tempting way. But he knew she wasn't asking to be kissed again.

'Thanks for dinner,' he said.

'Sure, no problem. Thanks for bringing the tree.'

He glanced at it and agreed that its cheer did something nice for Jenny's apartment. His gaze dwelled for a moment on the glittering star on top. He liked what it

180

represented, a symbol of hope, like the twinkling stars in the firmament that he liked to talk to when he felt most in communication with the universe. Silly notion to occur to him now. But maybe not so silly. Jenny had the ability to reach into his most sentimental parts.

They gazed at each other for a moment, the attraction between them still humming like a seductive melody. But they had too many lines to cross. He raised a hand in a gesture of parting.

'See you,' he said.

'Yes,' she replied.

Jenny closed the door and leaned on it. That had been a close call. She relived the thrilling sensations he'd elicited from her treacherous body and closed her eyes to listen to the tug of her heartstrings.

Then she pushed herself away from the door to tidy up the kitchen. When she got there, she had to rest her hands on the counter and brace herself, imagining the scent of his masculine essence still there.

'It can't be,' she said to herself with a sigh. 'Not now, anyway.'

Too much hung on how she handled things during the next few weeks. Probably a good thing. It would keep her from falling under Parker McAllister's spell. An affair with him would only end in another broken heart. It was too risky.

'Back to work,' she commanded her trembling, disobedient hands. She needed to be completely in control when Grace brought Roger home.

8

Sunday morning, Jenny fought off Parker invading her dreams again and indulged in a long, hot shower. Although Sunday was supposed to be a day of rest, it didn't seem that way anymore, especially in the hectic holiday season. She made breakfast for Roger and questioned him relentlessly about what homework remained to be done before school the next day.

She determined that he'd had enough computer games last night and decided she would take him Christmas shopping with her in the afternoon. She needed to get in her aerobics workout today, too.

'Roger,' she said as he was stuffing pancakes down his throat, 'how would you like to come to my step aerobics class with me?'

He chewed silently, observing her through his plastic-framed glasses. 'You mean one of those classes where women in sweatshirts go up and down on a green step?'

'Well, sort of. It's fun, Roger. You can learn the routines and sweat.'

He made a face at that. 'Why should I have to sweat?'

'Because aerobic exercise is good for you. It's only for an hour.' She gave him a sly grin. 'And they play loud music.'

He took another bite, watching her suspiciously. 'Then we're going shopping?'

'That's right. We can shower in the dressing rooms after the class. Then I'll take you to the mall.'

Roger rolled his eyes upward and lifted his arms in a gesture of surrender. 'Do I have a choice?'

'Well, not exactly.'

★   ★   ★

An hour later, Jenny and Roger were bouncing around in the step aerobics class to the pounding beat of music. The instructor, Angie, was good at calling out the steps in advance, and Jenny knew most of the routines. But there was little she could do about Roger inventing his own steps, yanking his arms up and down and galloping around the step. Angie corrected him when it looked like he was in danger of hurting himself. Otherwise, the other women and the few males in the class found Roger's antics amusing.

At the end of the class, Jenny felt sore but invigorated. Roger had worked up a sweat as well, and after putting their equipment away, she thanked Angie and guided Roger back to the men's dressing room.

'Don't dawdle in there,' she told him as she handed him a towel. 'Just shower off and get dressed. I'll meet you out here in fifteen minutes.'

'No problem.'

Feeling somewhat satisfied that she was living up to her baby-sitting responsibilities, she went into the women's dressing room, where she stripped down and then stepped into a deliciously warm shower. The tingling combination of exercised muscles and hot water soothing them reminded her of Parker's touch. Lord, was there no way she could get that man out of her mind?

Of course today he'd be working at the Christmas tree lot. Weekends in December would be a busy time for him. What was Sydney doing today? Was she at the lot again with him? Jenny puckered a brow, wondering if the little girl had any homework to do. She hoped Parker didn't overlook such an important part of parental responsibility.

'None of my business,' she told herself, massaging the warm water through her scalp.

Surprisingly, it became her business after their shopping trip to the mall. She and Roger came home with a bundle of packages.

They'd played the game of letting him pick out things he might like. Then, while he was playing in the video arcade, she made some purchases to put under the tree for him. She also finished her shopping for her parents. She would need to wrap the gifts today and mail them tomorrow.

By midafternoon, she threatened to withhold food from Roger until he dragged out what homework he needed to finish before tomorrow. When he reluctantly produced his math book, she got an idea.

'I need to check on some things in my office,' she told him. 'Why don't you bring your pack and work there for a little while? You can use the big round table in the marketing room while I organize some stuff on my desk.'

He screwed up his eyes at her. 'You work on Sunday?'

'Well, not usually, of course. But with so many things going on this month and some important visitors coming next week, I have some catching up to do.'

Roger acquiesced, and Jenny felt like maybe, just maybe, she wasn't doing such a bad job as a baby-sitter.

They crossed the parking lot and wended through the halls of the retirement home. Many of the elderly residents stopped to say hello, and she was surprised at how many of them commented on his tuba playing of Friday evening.

'Enjoyed your music, young man,' said Mr. Churchill.

'Thanks.'

'Looking forward to another program soon,' commented Mrs. Callahan.

Jenny got her young charge settled at the big round conference table in their marketing area. This was where she met with families and potential residents. The Formica top was edged in oak, and she wouldn't have to worry about Roger writing on the indestructible top.

Soon she was engrossed in paperwork, feeling some satisfaction in getting ahead of the game. An hour later she was ready to print out some reports to fax to corporate headquarters. Let them know she'd been working on a Sunday to make sure everything was done. Efficiency and dedication were two ingredients that might convince them that she could save this place. And it did look like she was going to show enough profit this month to placate them. And keep Cherry Valley Retirement Home afloat.

She glanced up to see a small person peeking around her door and jumped, her hand covering her heart.

'Oh, Sydney,' she said, as soon as she

recognized the little dark-haired girl. 'I didn't see you. You startled me. Come in.'

The girl slid the rest of her small body around the door jamb and came into the room cautiously.

'I didn't mean to scare you.'

'I know you didn't.'

Jenny smiled at her visitor. 'Are you visiting your grandmother today?'

The brunette ponytails wagged as she tilted her head back and forth. It was neither a yes nor a no, but Jenny guessed Sydney decided that the gesture most appropriately answered the question.

'Sort of,' said Sydney, taking a few more steps toward the desk.

She stopped when she was between the two guest chairs and rested a hand on the top of the one to her right. 'Daddy has to work today, so I stayed here.'

'Oh, I see.'

Jenny leaned her forearms on her desk and hunched forward. 'Would you like to have a seat?'

Sydney considered the gray upholstered chair and then looked back at Jenny warily.

'Okay. I guess so.'

Jenny waited while Sydney climbed up on the chair and then sat with legs dangling, feet not touching the floor. The sight of so young a person in a chair normally inhabited by those three times her size tickled some warm spot in Jenny's heart and she relaxed. It was time to take a break anyway. And visiting with Sydney seemed like a good excuse. She also realized that she wondered more about the little girl than perhaps she should, just because she was Parker McAllister's daughter.

'So what are you and Granny doing today?' Jenny began.

Sydney shrugged. 'She read to me, but I got bored with that. I've read all the stories myself anyway.'

'Oh, so you are a great reader?'

'Yeah, I guess so.'

'Well, that's good. That means you are well-equipped to learn a lot.'

'Hmmmm.'

Jenny began to sense there was something on the girl's mind and struggled with how to ask. She straightened up and twisted to the side, realizing her muscles had been in the same position for a long time.

She grunted as her muscles seemed to crackle, especially after the morning's class. 'Um, a stretch feels good.'

Sydney's eyes were directed toward Jenny's computer screen.

Taking her cue from that, Jenny inquired,

'Do you know how to work a computer?'

'Sure. We have them in school.'

Still the round, aquamarine eyes didn't reveal what was ticking inside. Jenny half turned in her swivel chair.

'Would you like to see what I'm doing?'

An enthusiastic nod of the head. Ah, that was it: She wanted to use the computer. Jenny was aware that kids were computer literate these days at a very young age. Sydney was probably just curious about Jenny's work. She grinned at the little girl and motioned for her to come around the desk.

'Well, come on. I'll get another chair and show you what I'm doing.'

Sydney hopped off the chair. Jenny brought a wooden folding chair from the side of the room and rolled her own chair to one side so the two of them could sit companionably side by side.

'This is accounting,' she explained, pointing to the spreadsheet with all its cells and numbers.

With Sydney as a rapt listener, Jenny was soon launched on a detailed explanation of the costs of running the retirement home. She went slowly at first, making sure she didn't use any words that Sydney couldn't grasp. And she stopped to define anything the little girl wanted to know. But she found that

Sydney was a quick pupil, and the comprehension once a term was defined brightened her eyes. Jenny soon knew the pleasure of teaching a young person and watching her excitement when she grasped new concepts. Sydney had an affinity for numbers, just as Jenny did, and it warmed her heart to find they had something in common.

The time passed enjoyably, and Jenny actually got a little more work done just by showing Sydney what she was doing. She chuckled over some of Sydney's perceptive questions about ordering supplies. Sydney even wanted to know where in the home the bulk supplies were kept.

'Why, Sydney,' Jenny said after about a half hour of going over her spreadsheet, 'I think you have an aptitude for accounting. Are you good at math in school?'

The little girl flopped her ponytails up and down vigorously. 'I'm in the top class. I always get A's in math.'

'That's great. So you're a good reader and good at math, too. You have a bright future ahead, my girl.'

Warmth infused Jenny as she and the little girl bonded in camaraderie. Jenny had never given much thought to having children of her own. Not having found the right man in her life yet, the issue of children seemed moot.

Now she felt an embarrassing warmth creep into her face as she remembered what had transpired between herself and Sydney's father. Surely if they continued in that vein, they would be well on the way to what brings children into this world, if they weren't careful.

A question burned into her mind. In spite of all the obstacles between them, would she be able to hold back if Parker decided to make love to her? Would they take the plunge? She allowed the fantasy to flit through her mind, but then struggled to discipline herself to make it go away. It wasn't practical. But it was getting harder and harder to do what was practical, though she had to remember that her job and the survival of Cherry Valley Retirement Home came first. She cleared her throat, focusing once again on the numbers on the screen.

'I'm going to tell the computer to print a report now, so I can turn it in to my bosses.'

Sydney wrinkled her brow. 'I thought you were the boss.'

'I'm the boss here,' she said with a grin. 'But this place is owned by a big company that has its headquarters in Chicago. I have to turn in reports to them so they know I'm doing a good job.'

'Are you doing a good job?'

'I hope so.'

Sydney watched with interest as Jenny merged the data into a report she could fax. The printer hummed and clicked, and then the report appeared.

'Do you want to help me fax this?' Jenny asked.

'Mmm-hmmm,' said Sydney, who slid off her chair and followed Jenny to the fax machine.

Jenny told her what numbers to punch into the machine, and then they watched the display as it told them the connection was being made. Soon the report was sucked into the machine, and then pushed out the other side.

'There,' said Jenny. 'All done.'

Sydney considered her with round, serious eyes. 'Can we do that for Daddy?'

'What?'

Sydney wandered back to her seat in front of computer. 'This,' she said, pointing to the spreadsheet on the screen. 'Can we make one of these for Daddy?'

Jenny didn't quite know what Sydney meant, but she came back to sit down beside her.

'Oh, you mean make a spreadsheet for your father's business?'

'Yes.'

'Well, he might not want us to do that. He probably has a system of his own. Does he have a computer at home?'

Sydney nodded solemnly. 'Yes, but he never has it on.'

'Well, he probably doesn't like to work when you're there. He probably does his accounting during the week, while you're in school.'

Jenny suddenly felt as if she was wandering into quicksand. Parker's business practices weren't any of her concern. But Sydney seemed so intent on it, Jenny felt obligated to find out what the little girl was so concerned about.

Sydney slid her fingers across the edge of Jenny's keyboard. 'Couldn't we figure out how much money he makes from selling the Christmas trees?'

Jenny's mouth parted in shocked surprise. 'Um, money?'

'Yeah, like how many trees does he sell, and how much does he make?'

'Uh, well, I don't know. Don't you think you should ask your daddy that?'

'Maybe.'

Jenny's head spun. What was going on here? She had no right to stick her nose into Parker's business this way, and yet the disappointment on Sydney's face that she wasn't going to get her answer was hard to ignore. Maybe there was a way to compromise.

'Well, uh, maybe we could look at a hypothetical scenario. Hypothetical means made-up conditions. It wouldn't really show what your daddy makes, but it would be an example. Like you do in math class. All right?'

Sydney nodded, her enthusiasm returning. So Jenny opened a new file and started to formulate the problem, setting up a table to represent the days of the week and the numbers of trees sold in each price category. Soon, she and Sydney were embarked on another mathematical adventure, giggling at the inventive ways they could price their trees. It would actually be the way she might set up a profit-and-loss projection if she were to open a business similar to Parker's. She wondered if he had done one.

Sydney clapped her hands when the computer calculated their profits for a week and then a month. She insisted they make a report and then print it out. Jenny handed it to her, and the little girl scanned it avidly.

Then her round eyes found Jenny's again, and she asked, 'Is this enough to live on?'

Jenny gulped. 'I, uh, well, that would depend.'

'On what?' Sydney asked with a frown.

Oh, Lord, she knew where this was headed now, and she wished she hadn't gotten involved. Sydney was trying to find out how much money her daddy made. But was there a specific reason for her question that Jenny wasn't yet understanding? Perhaps there was more to ferret out here than appeared.

'Let's sit down,' she said.

She pulled out one of the remaining wooden folding chairs at the round table where she conducted informal meetings. Sydney climbed onto her chair, placing the computer report in front of her. Jenny realized with chagrin that Sydney was going to want to take that report home. Then Parker would think . . . Uh-oh. She really didn't want to go there.

'Sydney,' she said, 'if you're worried about how much money your daddy makes, that's between you and him. It's not any of my business.'

Sydney rounded her eyes at Jenny. 'But you know how to do this stuff.'

'So does your daddy. He was an executive in a big electronics firm, honey. Remember?'

Sydney dropped her eyes. 'I know. But he doesn't ever talk about that. All he wants to talk about is me.'

'Well, that's because he loves you. He cares about your life.'

Up came the soulful blue eyes again. 'Then why can't I come and live with him?'

Zing went another arrow into Jenny's heart. She was at once honored that Sydney would confide in her and worried that she shouldn't be talking about these things behind Parker's back. It seemed dishonest and conniving somehow. But Sydney was a child; she wouldn't understand that. She was at the age when a kid just said what was on her mind.

Jenny gave an inward chuckle. Adults should be more like that sometimes. She struggled on this unfamiliar ground and tried to come up with a satisfactory answer.

'Well, I don't know what the arrangements are with your mother. She loves you, too, so she wants you to live with her.'

Sydney squirmed. 'Daddy's more fun.'

'Oh, he is? Well, I see.' She exhaled a breath and decided honesty was the best policy here. 'Listen, Sydney, I really don't know these answers. You should ask your parents. Does your daddy know you want to live with him?'

'Hmmmm. I think so.' Then Sydney confronted Jenny again with those insightful turquoise eyes. 'But if he can't sell Christmas trees after Christmas is over, how can he afford to take care of me?'

Jenny's heart wrenched. So this whole

financial exercise rested on Sydney's worry that her father wouldn't be able to support her. A question Jenny knew in her bones was important. A question any sensible woman would ask herself as well before she considered a relationship with such a man. She felt her inner machinery click and snap as more than one piece of the scenario fell into place.

Parker McAllister was a lovable man, a man who could strum Jenny's inner music a little too adeptly. But his winning personality and fun-loving way with kids might be the characteristics of a man who was a bit too fun-loving. Where in Parker's life did the word *responsibility* fit in?

She stared back at Sydney, stunned again by the depth of perception that could be found from a child's simple questions.

'I don't know, Sydney,' she said, realizing she was answering a question for herself as well. 'I don't know what he plans to do for a living after Christmas.'

★   ★   ★

It was almost suppertime when Parker learned from his mother that Sydney had gone to visit Jenny in her office. He wound through the basement hallways and took the staircase nearest the front lobby. He heard the soft voices of his daughter and the general manager talking in her office and was about to interrupt them when their words made him pause. In that split second that he halted behind the door, he heard what they were talking about.

Indignant emotion quickly turned to angry resentment. He couldn't believe Jenny had the nerve to talk to his daughter about what he did for a living. It unnerved him and humiliated him at the same time. He clenched his jaw. But then he steadied himself with a breath before he burst in on them.

Not that he minded accusing Jenny of sticking her nose into his business. That was bad enough, but to bring Sydney into it was unthinkable. He should have known better. He'd known she was full of strict, controlling ideas and obsessed by budgets. He'd warned himself that if he let her any deeper into his life, she would try to strangle him. But he'd been tempted to take the risk, tempted by a softness and light in her that he had sworn only needed a little kindling to burn bright.

He'd been wrong. He drew a deep breath before striding in to retrieve his daughter from Jenny's clutches.

9

Jenny's heart nearly stopped beating when Parker sailed through the door. She could see from the glower on his handsome face that he'd heard what they'd been saying. How much? Her leaden heart dropped to her toes and her throat constricted.

'Hi, Daddy,' said Sydney, unperturbed that she'd just been discussing her father's finances with a stranger.

'Hi, chicken,' he said, with only minimal warmth replacing the disgruntled expression on his face.

Oh, boy, Jenny thought. How was she going to extricate herself from this one? Before she could even get up, Sydney slid the report off the table and handed it to her father.

'See? Jenny's teaching me accounting. This is a report we did.'

Parker continued to stare daggers at Jenny as he took the report from Sydney's hands. His eyes swept over it and his mouth turned into a solid line. Feeling returned to Jenny, but in the form of abject embarrassment. She wished there were a large hole in the floor she could conveniently drop into.

'Uh, it was just an exercise. Sydney wanted to . . . to speculate.'

He grunted, and she could see him struggling to control any display of anger in front of his daughter. Finally, he let two words escape his tight lips. 'I see.'

Sydney crushed one edge of his jacket in her hand and then twisted her body around. But she wasn't anxious. Jenny could tell that the little girl's mind was ready to move on to other things. She stopped her wiggling and tilted her head back to look up at her dad.

'I'm hungry. Isn't it dinnertime yet?'

Parker lifted one dark eyebrow and thrust the report back onto the table. Evidently, he wasn't going to encourage his daughter to take it home.

'You're right, chicken. It's time to go eat. What would you like to eat tonight?'

Sydney made a face. 'I don't want stroganoff again. Mine was mushy.'

Parker pulled down a corner of his lips. 'Don't worry, we're not staying here for dinner. We'll go somewhere where they don't even have stroganoff on the menu.'

He gave Jenny one last glance as his hand moved Sydney toward the door. Then he turned. Jenny stood like a stone, horrified and humiliated. But Sydney remembered her manners. At the door, she turned and ducked around her dad.

'Bye,' she said to Jenny.

'Bye, Sydney,' Jenny said with a hoarse throat.

Parker said nothing, only ushered his daughter out.

Jenny moved toward the door but didn't watch them leave. She heard their voices drift down the hall. At least Parker was enough in control of himself not to be angry with Sydney. That was something to be glad for. No, it was Jenny who would come under fire. At least he was going to place the blame where it belonged.

She strode back to her desk and slowly lowered herself into the chair. Suddenly she wanted to cry. What an awful mess. He would never forgive her. Never in her life had she felt so terrible. It looked like she'd been pumping Sydney for information about Parker's income.

'Damn!' she said, squeezing a fist down on the desk. Damn and double damn. How could she ever explain? And yet she couldn't risk butting in again. It had been Sydney who'd led her down the primrose path, but if Jenny tried to point that out to Parker, it would intrude on his relationship with his daughter. Jenny didn't want to get in the middle of a father-daughter discussion that was so personal. Why had she listened to Sydney? Why hadn't she cut her off when she'd started to talk about Christmas trees?

Sinking into self-pity, Jenny let a sob escape. Well, better get it out of her system. A good cry might be just the thing. She moaned and choked out another sob and then let it come, getting some wracking-good crying done.

It was over in a minute or two, but she was still pacing the office and wiping her eyes and nose with tissues when Grace walked in.

The other woman stopped suddenly, halfway into the office, her mouth a round *O*, her eyes wide with concern. Grace's gaze flew from Jenny to the desk; then her eyes opened wider. She approached the desk hesitantly and squinted at the accounting report Jenny had printed and faxed to headquarters.

'My gosh,' said Grace. 'Is it that bad?'

'No, no,' Jenny said, gasping for restorative breaths. 'I'm not crying over that.'

Grace's hand flew to her heart in relief.

'Oh, you had me scared. I thought maybe we were going under tomorrow. I haven't had time to look for another job.'

Jenny allowed herself a few more shaky breaths to get herself back to normal, and as she did so, she went to her chair behind the desk again. It seemed the most secure place, although she was well aware that that was just an illusion.

'We're not done for yet,' she said. She could be fairly honest with Grace about their situation. 'Everything hinges on the inspection,' she said. 'But I think I've tightened up the budget sufficiently. If we're lucky, we'll still have jobs next month.'

She took deep breaths as Grace dropped her coat and shopping bags on the floor, then sat down in one of the gray upholstered chairs. For a moment, neither spoke as Jenny tried to put on her professional face. But Grace's perceptive gaze penetrated her facade.

'Hmmmmm. Then if you don't mind my asking, what happened to cause this upset? Has someone said something insulting?'

Jenny met Grace's inquiring gaze with a self-recriminating one of her own.

'Yes. Me.'

To ease Grace's puzzlement, she continued. 'I suppose you could call it a misunderstanding. But I've made Parker, um, mad.'

She sighed, wanting to unburden herself and hoping Grace would understand.

'Sydney came in while I was working on the spread-sheet. One thing led to another, and pretty soon we were doing an analysis on how much money her father could make selling Christmas trees. I didn't mean to stick my nose into their business. It just happened.'

'Ohhhh,' Grace said as enlightenment dawned. 'I just saw him leading Sydney toward the pickup truck. I thought he looked rather as if he'd just met up with Osiris from the Underworld.'

Grace shook her head, and Jenny could feel the other woman's sympathy.

'I think there is something that has occurred between you and our Parker McAllister. Correct me if I'm wrong. Did he . . . express an interest last night?'

Grace's goodwill and her gracious surrender where Parker was concerned warmed Jenny, and she wanted to squeeze her friend's hand in appreciation. But she wasn't given to expressions of affection, so she just gave her a regretful smile.

'I'm afraid things have gotten out of hand between us. Now, doubly so.'

Jenny cleared her throat and straightened her back. 'I'm afraid I've weakened, Grace. I've started to have unruly thoughts about the man, and I don't know what to do with them.'

Grace gave a tigerlike *grrrrr* in her throat and winked. 'You should do what any healthy, single female would do.'

'But I can't. It might mean my job.'

'Oh, I had forgotten about that.'

'Anyway, now that he thinks I'm a nosy, interfering bitch, the matter will be closed. It's better that way. I need to concentrate on my job.'

Grace's brows wrinkled. 'You always do that, boss lady. I'd think you might want to concentrate on other things once in a while.'

Jenny sighed again. 'I will, after this blasted Christmas season is over.'

'That bad, is it? I had thought we brought you some cheer last night.'

'You did, and I appreciate it. Oh, gosh. I forgot Roger. He's in the conference room doing homework. I'd better go get him and prepare to feed the gaping maw.'

Shoving the personal disaster aside as much as she could, Jenny pushed herself up from the desk and confronted the realities of her life.

★   ★   ★

Parker realized Sydney must have felt the silence. Instead of joking with her and creating a warm, trusting environment, he barely spoke on the way home. Seeing his daughter and Jenny speculating about his personal income had been a blow way below the belt. He was still astonished that Jenny could be that manipulative. He would refrain from talking about it with Sydney until they'd gotten home and had had something to eat. By then, maybe the rage that seethed just below the surface would be mitigated.

After cooking a frozen pizza and letting Sydney help him cut up vegetables for a salad, they drew up their chairs to the kitchen table.

'So tell me what you did at Grandma's,' he began.

After swallowing a mouthful, Sydney replied, 'We read. Then she showed me some pictures of when she was a little girl. They wore funny clothes then.'

He grunted an acknowledgment as he chewed.

'What made you decide to go see Miss Knight?'

'I dunno. I was bored, I guess. Grandma said it would be all right if I took a walk, long as I stayed in the building.'

'I see.'

He ate another slice of pizza, deciding how best to tackle the problem. 'Honey, were you talking to Jenny about how I run my business?'

Sydney tilted her head from side to side,

wiggling in her chair. 'Not 'zactly.'

'What 'zactly' were you talking about?'

'Well, I just wondered how many trees you'd have to sell to . . . ' Her voice faded off and she stared down at her plate.

'To what?'

'To take care of me,' she finally said, sitting up but not looking at him.

Daggers struck Parker's heart. He thought eight years old was too young for a child to worry about money. Evidently he was wrong. He reached out and touched her hand with his.

'Honey, I'll always take care of you. You don't have to worry about that.'

Now she looked up at him with something like confusion on her perky face. The simmering anger started to boil inside him again, and he knew whom to blame this time.

'Sydney, has your mother been talking to you about how I make a living?'

Up and down went the thin shoulders. 'Maybe, but I don't listen to her about things like that.'

His eyebrows raised. 'You don't? Then who do you listen to?'

'No one. It's just that . . . '

'What, honey?'

'I want to come live with you.'

Parker opened his mouth to say something,

but the words were stopped by the emotion that gathered in his throat. He reached over and picked Sydney up to pull her onto his lap for a hug.

Emotion tugged at him, and his eyes moistened. He didn't want to overwhelm Sydney with an emotional scene, but when she wrapped her arms around his neck and returned the hug, he thought his heart would break. Finally, he set Sydney away from him on his knee so he could look at her.

'I'd love to have you live with me,' he said when he could manage to speak. 'But your mom wants you too.'

Sydney wagged her ponytails. 'I dunno. She's busy all the time. She and Mel go out a lot.' Melville was Sheila's husband.

He inhaled a long, slow breath and then let it go.

'Tell you what; I'll talk to your mother about this. She might not feel I would do a very good job as both a mother and a father.'

Sydney stretched her arm out onto the table and walked her fingers idly across a quilted place mat. 'You could get a new mom for me, then.'

Parker's dark brows lifted. Amusement and consternation filled him.

'Oh, just go down to the shopping mall and pick one out.'

'No. I'm not stupid. I know that's not how you do it.'

'I see. Well . . . ' He cleared his throat. 'How do you do it?'

'You know.' She poked him in the chest. 'You take her out on a date first.'

Parker's jaws locked. Now he knew what was going on. He was being manipulated into a corner by both Jenny and his daughter. He would do anything for Sydney, but there were limits on what she could demand of his personal life. He set her back onto the floor so she could get back onto her chair.

'Honey, I think you'd better leave it to me who I take out on a date. I don't think I'm ready to have another woman in my life.'

'Why not?'

Why did kids have to be so persistent? He crossed his arms and leaned back in his chair. 'Because some women want to rule your life.'

Sydney screwed up her mouth and drew invisible figures on the table with her fingers while she thought about that. Parker hunkered over again.

'But I want you to know, hon, that I'll always be able to take care of you. Money isn't a problem. I'm sorry if you were worried about that. I don't have to depend on the Christmas trees for my living.'

She looked up at him suspiciously. 'What'd

you do? Rob a bank?'

He grinned. 'No, I didn't rob a bank. But I do have some money put away to take care of us until I find a job after the holidays. Now, young lady, I want you to put all such worries out of your head.'

She looked as if she might be convinced at last. But as they did the dishes, Parker did some soul-searching. It bothered him that women like Jenny — and his daughter for that matter — seemed to want to do a financial background check on him. What he really wanted was a woman who could believe in him without always having to have explanations. His earlier suspicions were confirmed: No such woman existed.

Later that night, after Sydney was tucked in bed, Parker opened a bottle of Moosehead beer and watched the news in his den. But he found himself flipping channels, barely listening to the news. Images of rescue workers digging through collapsed buildings after an earthquake in the Philippines barely registered. Finally, he flipped the TV off and sat staring at the empty screen. He didn't turn to alcohol for comfort as a rule, and having a beer alone in his darkened den only made him feel more isolated.

He wanted to ignore Jenny Knight and her nosy interference, but something told him he would have to confront her. Not right away. Maybe after a week away from her, he wouldn't be so foolish as to be tempted by her sexy beauty and urge that had almost overcome him to loosen her up. She had loosened up plenty in his arms in her kitchen. One more minute and his hands and lips would have crossed the boundaries.

Thinking about it now made his groin tighten. Damn, she made him want her. He'd wanted to lean her on that kitchen stool and take her right there last night. And she'd wanted it, too. Some part of her wasn't all rigid and knotted up by company policy and bottom lines. Some part of her longed for the freedom to express herself. He had to gulp another sip of beer, contemplating what it would be like to make love to her. Turn her loose to glory in exquisite passion.

But he shook his head. Where was his mind going? Maybe this side of Jenny that he fantasized about was only a figment of his imagination. If she did give way to passion once, she might instantly regret it. He wouldn't want to see recriminations in those lovely brown eyes. And he couldn't abide a controlling woman. What he'd heard her discussing with Sydney was strictly off-limits; he wasn't about to weaken on that point. He was through with women who had to put him under a microscope. Even if he felt a twinge of disappointment that Jenny was turning out to be such a woman.

He slugged back the beer and attempted to focus on the news again, commanding his body to cease the longing it felt for one special woman. Instead he focused his determination on Sydney's wish to come and live with him. He'd love nothing more, if he could work out the details with Sheila. And his mother might be willing to watch Sydney after school until he came to pick her up for dinner each night.

Parker warmed to the possibilities. Christmas would be over in another couple of weeks, and it would be time to start thinking about a real job. One that would allow time for family. But he was doing it for himself and his little girl. No woman would ever dictate the circumstances of his life again.

★　★　★

Wednesday morning, Jenny faced a gathering of the residents for an information meeting in the commons room. She'd been as relaxed and friendly as she could be, greeting them as they came in. But it was Grace Douglas who made their eyes sparkle. Jenny envied her friend's easygoing, compassionate nature. But as the captain of this ship, it was Jenny's job to deliver both good news and bad.

She was aware that residents in a retirement home were never going to be 100 percent happy. Her mind flew back to Parker's complaint that his mother had to eat too much chocolate. She had instructed the chef to see that more varied items were on the menu now. But for every complaint resolved, there were eighty-nine more.

She tried to show these people that she liked them. But no one understood the thin line she walked, nor her dedication to keeping a roof over their silver and gray heads. Thinking that she might fail in that effort brought a swelling to her throat. She couldn't fail, for her grandmother's sake as well as her own. One more failure would do her in.

She gritted her teeth at that last thought. She had failed in her relationship with Drake; she had failed miserably on Sunday with Parker's daughter. Maybe she just didn't possess the people skills needed for a close and nurturing relationship, let alone such a people-type job as this one. But now was hardly the time to think of that. She had a meeting to conduct.

'Good morning,' she said, when most of her flock was settled in chairs gathered in rows for the meeting.

A few voices replied. In the back of the room, Jenny saw Grace bringing more chairs and helping to settle some gentlemen there, making sure the rolling oxygen tanks were out of the way. Nurse's aides in their pink uniforms also dotted the gathering, making sure the more fragile residents found seats.

Jenny got everyone's attention and launched into her announcements, sticking to the upbeat things as much as she could. She introduced some new residents who had just moved in, and then announced the birthdays for the month. A special luncheon was held each month to honor the celebrants. Most of the faces blinked contentedly at her until she came to an item she knew would be controversial.

'One week from tomorrow, we've scheduled something new, a trip to the Denver Art Museum.'

She raised her hand, indicating that she'd like to get a count of participants. 'How many think they might like to go?'

Before the hands could mobilize upward, Mr. Mossback's wheezing voice assailed her from the front row. 'What happened to our gambling trip?'

Murmurs of inquiry followed that. Jenny had known this was coming, and she raised a palm to try to mollify them.

'I know you've all gone to Central City to gamble before, but with so many accidents on Highway Six in the past few months, we decided to postpone the gambling trip until next summer, when we can be sure of better weather.'

'We used to go every month,' grumbled Mrs. Seymour. Other grumbles accompanied hers.

Jenny smiled cheerily. 'Your safety comes first,' she chirped. 'The museum is in town and easier to get to.'

And saves gasoline and wear-and-tear on the bus, she thought silently. But she pushed on with arguments she hoped would sway them. 'There's a special exhibit of Fabergé eggs on loan from the Louvre. Doesn't that sound interesting?'

'I eat eggs for breakfast,' barked the large Mr. Mossback, his round belly protruding upward from where he leaned the rest of his body back on his metal folding chair.

Everyone else laughed. Jenny clenched her jaw but attempted to join in the humor.

'I know, Mr. Mossback, but there will be other things to see. The bus will be outside at one-thirty next Thursday, right after lunch. We'll be back in time for the five-thirty dinner seating. We'll have a sign-up sheet at the desk.'

216

Jenny quickly moved on to other business. She couldn't tell them that headquarters had dictated that they cancel the gambling trip. She wasn't about to entertain any more arguments.

During the last fifteen minutes of the meeting Jenny took general questions. By the time she was finished, she was wound tight as a spring, and after she adjourned the meeting, she snagged a cup of coffee from one of the carafes kept full and hot at the side of the room. She stayed to visit with one or two of the residents but sneaked away to the safe refuge of her office as soon as she could.

She wasn't aware that a cluster of residents remained for their morning coffee. And appointed themselves delegates to appeal to Dorothy McAllister about the situation when she returned from her doctor's appointment.

When Dorothy answered her door later that afternoon, she invited the little delegation into her apartment to fill her in on the meeting she'd had to miss. After all, these were members of the coffee klatch that met nearly every afternoon around three o'clock in any case.

'Dorothy,' began Mrs. Seymour, 'there's to be no gambling. We can't take the bus to Central City.'

'Oh, that's too bad,' replied Dorothy from

her comfortable rocking chair.

'They want to take us to the art museum instead,' said Mr. Mossback with a snort.

Dorothy turned her head in his direction. 'Well, that sounds nice.'

'But what about our gambling?' Mrs. Davis was a petite doctor's widow who'd always enjoyed gambling and could afford to lose.

Dorothy met the inquiring gazes of her friends. 'What am I supposed to do about it?'

'Ask your son.'

'Parker?'

'We know he calls Bingo. Didn't you say he used to call Bingo at the community center on Saturday nights when you lived in Heather Heights?'

'Why, yes, he did. You mean you'd like him to do that here?'

They nodded enthusiastically. 'We think that would be a great idea.'

★   ★   ★

Parker agreed to donate his afternoon off the following Thursday to his mother's Bingo game. He jotted it in his day planner and gave it no more thought. He'd been thankful for a busy week so far and had managed to keep his mind relatively free of his obsession with Jenny Knight. He did some work on the house in the early mornings before he reported to the Christmas tree lot, preparing it for Sydney's more permanent stay. He'd managed to talk to Sheila in one of her saner moments, and they'd agreed to work something out. After all, they both wanted Sydney to be happy. If she wanted to live with Dad for a while, Sheila could be accommodating. Parker sensed in her words that it would give her more time for her society benefits, which endeared her to the social set she so coveted.

By the time Friday afternoon rolled around, Parker congratulated himself on taking care of business. With some of the small things accomplished, the bigger ones would surely fall into place. Things would work out.

That was before he went to see his mother on Friday evening and walked past the open door to a supply room in the corridor on the way to her apartment. Jenny stood on a stepladder, examining cases of soap and marking something on a clipboard. She shook her head, muttered to herself and glanced up higher. The shelves were packed from floor to ceiling with cases, bottles and various packages. It had to have taken something taller than the stepladder to unload things onto the highest shelves.

Jenny stretched her arm upward, a finger straining for a box. Her hiked-up skirt revealed a sexy turquoise lace slip sliding along smooth taupe panty hose covering shapely thighs. A sight that would make even a strong man pause. And when she stretched too far and had to grasp the boxes of toilet tissue to regain her balance, Parker instinctively leapt forward to catch her in case she fell.

'You all right?' he queried, frowning up at her.

Shocked surprise registered on her face. Her wide brown eyes rounded, and her full, cranberry lips opened as she gasped.

'Oh, Parker, you startled me.'

One of her hands clutched the boxes and the other grasped the flimsy metal shelving. Her pen clattered to the floor.

He bent to pick it up, but when he came up again, he realized his mistake. His face passed near her legs, and he caught a whiff of her clean, fresh, tantalizing scent. He moved away a fraction and handed her the pen.

'Your balance looked a little precarious,' he said. 'You shouldn't climb up there dressed like that.'

Her breath was shallow, and she seemed to tremble slightly.

'I'm all right. I was just checking the inventory figures.'

He came around to her other side and gave her a hand to assist her descent.

He shouldn't have touched her. As soon as he did, he didn't want to let go, undermining all his fierce decisions about her. The breathless look on her face and the flush of her cheeks told him that she felt the spark that sizzled between them, filling them both with a heat that should have been against the law.

Then he did something even more foolish. Keeping hold of her with one hand, he took a step backwards so he could reach out and close the door.

10

They looked into each other's eyes for a long, hard minute while Parker's blood pressure reached boiling point. He'd thought he'd gotten her out of his system after a long, hard week at work and by preparing a home for his daughter. Yet even the memory that this was the woman who had fanned Sydney's curiosity about her father's income couldn't douse the physical attraction. But he'd be damned if he'd let any of it show before he gave her a piece of his mind. Then they both spoke simultaneously.

'I owe you an apology,' Jenny said.

'We need to talk,' said Parker at the same moment.

Then they both broke off and waited. Jenny lowered her head first.

'I know what it looked like the other day, and I wanted to explain . . . '

He looked above her head, trying to compose himself. Where was the stern lecture he'd been preparing to deliver? He reluctantly allowed her to draw her hand away.

'I've had a talk with Sydney,' he said.

'Have you?'

He couldn't interpret whether the hopeful expression on her face was for herself or for Sydney. It was the latter that he had to set some rules for. Still, the pained embarrassment swimming in Jenny's honey-brown eyes made him suddenly want to reassure her that it wasn't all her fault.

'I'm afraid Sydney asked you some questions that should have been kept in the family,' he grumbled, swiping a hand through his hair. 'She should have come to me.'

'Then you've . . . reassured her.'

He nodded, his body convulsing with conflicting desires. He'd come in here ready to put her in her place. But her humble apology unmanned him. He wanted to take her head between his hands and tilt it back, see her eyelids close so that the fingers of her lashes lay upon her cheeks. How was he ever going to keep from falling into this siren's trap?

She, in fact, batted those lashes most appealingly.

'I'm glad.' Her voice was warm. 'I didn't mean to interfere. I was pulled in by her questions. I'm sorry, if I . . . '

'Hmmmmm.' His acknowledgment interrupted her trailing words.

They were both staring at each other as if all the start-and-stop sentences in the world couldn't explain their feelings, feelings that roiled inside Parker in a most disconcerting way. He couldn't help but wonder what she would feel like in his arms again. Having had her against him once only made him want to experience it again. His rational mind was trying to remind him that she was nosy and controlling, that he didn't want that sort of woman in his life ever again. But there was a magnetism between them that wouldn't quit.

He was going to kiss her; he knew it. Right here in the supply closet. If she didn't want him to, there was the door. But she made no move toward it. Instead, her lips were parted and her head tilted back slightly. Some auburn locks of hair curled against her cheeks, and her eyelids half-covered her eyes. He could almost hear her heart pounding against her chest. And her shapely body, molded in a teal green turtleneck, was so damned sexy. Why did his traitorous fingers long to comb through her soft, springy hair?

'Jenny?' he murmured. But he couldn't think of exactly what to follow it up with.

'Uh,' she said, moistening her dry lips.

'Jenny,' he said again in a stronger voice.

This time he moved closer to her and took her elbows in his hands.

'You drive me crazy,' he finally admitted.

Her eyes came more fully open, and she

met his gaze full on. But it wasn't displeasure or bossiness he saw there. Instead her expressive brown eyes, laced with gold, gazed at him innocently, provocatively.

'I thought you said this was against the rules,' he said, sliding one hand around her waist as he pulled her against him so that her head had to move back farther.

'What?' she whispered on a breath.

'This.' And he kissed her with deliberation.

The week they'd been apart had only reminded him of how much he wanted this. Even if his life wasn't set up for it right now, his soul hungered for a partner as much as his body wanted a mate. So what if they were standing only a few feet from a public corridor? The hollow, particleboard door was enough to ensure their privacy. And now that his blood pulsed maddeningly, he couldn't let her go until he'd at least satisfied himself with an expression of his feelings. There were some things, he thought dimly, as he tasted her mouth once again, that just couldn't be put in a box. Passion was one of them.

Jenny responded to the kiss with an aching hunger. The guilt and regret she'd lived with all week were replaced with a rushing sense of relief that she'd seen Parker again at last. She hadn't said everything that she wanted to say, but he seemed to understand. Their instant connection had been enough. Now guilty joy replaced guilty regret, and she wrapped her arms around his firm torso and opened her mouth to his warm kiss. Soft moans emanated from the back of her throat, even as she realized that they needed to be quiet. This wasn't a place of guaranteed privacy.

When he released her lips and tantalized her ear with his lips and tongue, she whispered his name. She was doing exactly what she'd promised herself not to do. Was she such a fool then, helpless where it came to men? How her body wanted his touch. And when he slid a hand around to the front of her sweater to caress her breast, her knees went weak. Hot desire shot through her, and she knew that if they'd been in her apartment, she'd go much farther with him. Only their location protected her. Damn the rules, she thought to herself as her own hands found their way under his jacket. Damn everything except her need for this man.

Was this how it had been with Drake? She didn't think so. Her desire for Parker McAllister seemed to come from the inside. With Drake everything had come from the outside world. Money, fancy dates, luxurious surroundings. Lovemaking had simply been the programmed end of a well-orchestrated date. But as Parker moaned against her neck and pressed his hand against her buttocks, she knew how lost they were.

'Jenny,' he murmured gruffly. 'What are we going to do?'

She purred against his shoulder. 'I don't know.'

And then his mouth captured hers again and they continued their wild and frenzied reaching and searching. It seemed as if they couldn't get close enough to each other. Suddenly, she wanted to be next to his skin. They couldn't, of course, not here. But . . .

As if reading her thoughts, his hand reached down and lifted the hem of her slip. Suddenly, her panty hose seemed an insurmountable barrier. Good heavens, what was she thinking? What was she going to let him do? This was crazy.

Yes, it was crazy, she almost whispered aloud. But maybe that was what she needed. To be crazy, for once in her life, and worry about the rest later.

He swung her around and back into a small aisle at the end of the shelving along one wall that stopped a few feet short of some waist-high cardboard boxes. She hadn't realized the space was there. Somehow, Parker's hands had found their way under the waistband of the panty hose and were sliding them downward.

'I just want to feel your skin,' he whispered against her hair. 'I'll stop any time you want me to.'

But with her hands on the solid rod that bulged against his light tan cords, how could she plead that she wanted him to stop? Of course they would have to stop at some point. They couldn't do it *here*, but neither of them was ready to give up yet.

'Hmmm,' was all she said as he peeled her panty hose to her ankles. She stepped out of her shoes and kicked nylon aside. And then she rested her back against the wall as he kissed her ankles. Shivers raced up her legs as his hand slid up her calf, followed by his mouth. She never knew that the back of her knee could be such a sensitive spot.

'Oh, my God,' she said out loud as his lips climbed upward to her thigh.

Then he stood up, his mouth stopping to gently nuzzle her breast, while his fingers still trailed up her leg under her skirt. She was completely undone.

Delicious was the word that pounded in her mind. No one had ever done this to her. He was a master.

His kiss was harder and more demanding this time, and she massaged his body while his fingers played with her thin bikini underwear. They danced around to her buttocks, and then his hand cupped her behind so he could rock against her. There wasn't any doubt about what he wanted. But even he knew they couldn't strip naked and couple here between the laundry detergent and the cases of toilet paper. But their heavy breathing might have spoken otherwise.

However much Parker wanted her, he, too, must not have wanted their first joining to take place in such surroundings, although part of Jenny's mind got wicked satisfaction out of the daring idea. Was knowing Parker McAllister opening up new doors of daring, then?

He teased her lips with his tongue, but he unlaced his fingers from her underwear and withdrew his hands to rest comfortably against her buttocks with her skirt and slip safely smoothed down again.

'Jenny, go out with me,' he muttered. 'Let's make this official. I want a date.'

Mirth gurgled up to stanch her heated desire. 'A date?'

'Mmmmm,' he said. 'I want a real date, not just a few stolen moments. I can't fight you anymore. Go out to dinner with me so we can get acquainted.'

If what they'd just done wasn't getting acquainted, she didn't know what was! But she felt a pleased sort of gratification that he was being a gentleman, at least belatedly so.

'I suppose we have a lot to talk about,' she said in a hoarse whisper.

'Yes,' he said.

They playfully kissed and nuzzled each other, foreheads finally resting against each other as they righted their clothing.

'What will your residents think if you appear all flushed and rumpled coming out of the supply room?' he teased.

'Oh,' she groaned, realizing that some of them might have seen Parker come in here and seen the door shut. Just her luck, one of them might have been the spy.

She flushed scarlet as she smoothed her hair and clothing. She found everything else to look at rather than meet his gaze again. But he wasn't going to let her off so easily this time.

'What about that date?' he asked.

'Um, right.' He could tell she was ill at ease again.

'How about . . . ?' He stopped, grimacing. He didn't have any free time himself this weekend, between Sydney and the lot.

'I'll see if Gary can cover for me tomorrow night. Will that work for you?'

He placed his hands on her waist again, wanting to maintain the contact they'd just shared and to reassure her that he meant business. He sensed something of the scared rabbit in her. She might be drawn to him physically, but she was afraid to get involved. He couldn't blame her. He'd shied away from involvement himself until now. He lifted his fingers to graze her cheek.

'Um,' she said with her eyes half closed. 'Tomorrow night will be fine.'

'Good. I'll pick you up at your apartment. Sydney can spend the night at my mom's.'

Jenny's eyes flew open, startled. 'Oh, my gosh. I forgot Roger. I'll have to get a baby-sitter. I don't even know one.' She slumped. 'I don't think I can impose on Grace again.'

He gave her a sympathetic look. Between her nephew and his responsibilities, it seemed as if they didn't have a chance at privacy. And privacy was what they needed. He made a decision.

'I'll tell you what: I'll find a baby-sitter for you myself. If worse comes to worse, Roger and Sydney can entertain each other at my mother's until their bedtime. Sydney sleeps on a spare bed in Mom's study. Roger can watch TV in the living room.'

'We can't disrupt your whole family that way.'

It was a dilemma, he agreed, but right now he was determined to solve the logistics for just one evening with this woman.

'There will be a way,' he told her with determination. 'Seven o'clock, your apartment.'

Then he stepped away from her and reached for the door. He felt foolish, trying to sneak out of a supply closet like a guilty teenager. He grinned suddenly and reached for her hand.

'Come on. We'll go out together.'

'But . . .'

He raised his voice, beginning a serious conversation about the number of Christmas greens needed for the upcoming production. He spoke in a loud voice as he slowly opened the door.

'I'll deliver the greens for the balcony that morning. I should think you have enough red ribbon in that box over there to drape the railing with. You don't want to block the view of the stage.'

She joined him in the hall, focusing on his face, her own expression deadpan.

'Thank you, Mr. McAllister, for your estimate of what we need. I'll get back to you with that purchase order.'

He stuck out his hand to shake hers and felt her hand tremble in his, but he pumped it in a businesslike fashion. No one would ever guess that only moments before they'd been clasped together in the heat of passion, exploring each other with an explosive need. He was grateful that there wasn't anyone very near them in the corridor. Otherwise they might have seen the smoke in their eyes.

He turned from her and strode off toward his mother's apartment. He didn't need to hide his interest in Jenny from his mother, especially now that she was going to be called upon to baby-sit. He just hoped she wouldn't mind helping him out. Though he had a sneaking suspicion she would be delighted to do anything that would further her son's love life.

★   ★   ★

Jenny wobbled back to her office. What had she done? She couldn't believe herself so capable of losing control, and that was exactly what Parker McAllister made her do.

She made it to her desk, but it was ten minutes before she began to focus on the work on her computer screen. Well, they had a date for tomorrow night. They'd have to jump through hoops to get any time together, but she suspected he was as willing to do the jumping as she was. Maybe they would talk about the direction in which this explosive relationship was going. No, maybe not talk.

Maybe she just needed to take the plunge and get him out of her system. She'd fantasized about what it would be like to make love with him. Maybe she just needed to go ahead and do it.

She was under no illusions. He wanted her, but neither of them was ready for a relationship. So be it, then. Her lips curved in a lascivious grin. Just a night of indulgence. They were two consenting adults, unattached and available. Why not have a fling? At least it would satisfy her screaming hormones. So what if it wasn't for keeps? With her fast-paced life, maybe she didn't have time for anything to be for keeps. That way she wouldn't have to worry about his personal problems either.

'That's it, girl,' she said to herself. She would look forward to a champagne and chocolate mousse evening. Lovemaking until they made the floors shake.

And then they would have to get dressed so she could come home to pick Roger up from the baby-sitter and act like the respectable aunt she considered herself to be. She got a pad of paper and made a shopping list. Since Parker got off work late, she didn't want to waste time going out to dinner. She would cook. If Dorothy McAllister was really willing to baby-sit, they could spend the evening at her apartment dining and ... She would touch base with him tomorrow morning about their plans.

★ ★ ★

After ordering Roger to take a bath on Saturday afternoon, Jenny stuffed Roger with as much spinach lasagne as she could get him to eat. Then, after making sure he changed into a sweatshirt without tomato stains, she walked him over to Dorothy McAllister's at seven o'clock. Dorothy had called her to say she'd be more than happy to have Roger stay for the evening.

'Don't worry, Jenny. He can watch late-night movies in my living room as long as he keeps it low. He'll probably fall asleep on the couch.'

Jenny had stumbled over her thanks, embarrassed at the implications that Parker's mother was keeping the kids so Jenny and Parker could be alone together. But there was a bit of the matchmaker in Dorothy, Jenny decided. The older woman's voice was warm with generosity.

Now she marched Roger along the hallway, pleased that they'd accomplished so much today. She'd shopped again while he was at his music lesson, and afterward, he'd diligently finished his homework. Armed now with his chessboard and pieces and the two movies Jenny had rented for the kids to watch, surely he and Sydney wouldn't run out of things to do. And Dorothy would keep them from fighting.

She plastered a nervous smile on her face as she lifted the knocker on Dorothy's door, then waited, her hands on Roger's shoulders.

The older woman greeted them, dressed elegantly as usual in gray wool slacks and a white cotton sweater. Silver earrings and necklace complemented her attractive face. Jenny admired the fact that some women maintained their grace and sophistication into their golden years.

'Come in, dear. Hello, Roger,' said Dorothy.

Roger marched in and placed his game and the movies on Dorothy's coffee table. Jenny noted that she'd covered it with a sturdy pink plastic cloth. Wise for an evening ahead with two rambunctious kids.

'We brought two movies. I hope you and Sydney will enjoy them if you decide to watch.'

'That sounds fine. I'm looking forward to it.'

Dorothy smiled contentedly at Jenny. Was that a twinkle of hope in her blue eyes?

Scanning the living room, she saw that Sydney wasn't there. Parker must be planning to drop her off just before coming over for dinner. She smiled shakily at Dorothy.

'I appreciate your willingness to do this. It's above and beyond the call of duty.'

Dorothy gave her an assessing look. 'Sometimes there are more important things than duty.'

Jenny's eyes widened. Was there a subtle message in that?

'We shouldn't be too late,' she hastened to say.

'Don't worry. You have a good time.' She gave Jenny a wink. 'I'll make sure the kids don't tear each other's hair out.'

Jenny chuckled. 'Thanks.'

She fled back to her apartment, knowing for sure that she was crazy. She was breaking her self-imposed rules, and the entire coffee klatch would soon know that she had a date with a resident's son. Headquarters would probably find out about it too. That galled her, but she was beginning to resent having to live her life with such tight strictures. Parker McAllister was making her live dangerously.

She wanted to believe that she wouldn't do it if it in any way endangered the residents of the retirement home. Come next weekend, she believed that when the corporate team arrived, they would find her accounting impeccable, her inventories exact and the residents well cared for. They might fire her for fraternization, but they wouldn't — couldn't — close the doors.

After tonight, discipline would return to her life. She didn't expect anything more from Parker. A frenzied affair, perhaps, an aberration of the holiday spirit. But she wasn't looking for commitment because she didn't think she could bring herself to depend on a man ever again. From here on out, Jenny Knight would depend on herself alone.

By the time she had the table set, her special spaghetti sauce simmering on the stove, and had made a quick check of her makeup and hair, she felt breathless. When the doorbell rang, she approached it as jittery as a teenager. And when Parker stepped in, carrying two bottles of wine in a sturdy paper bag with handles, she felt a tingling rush of excitement from her fingertips to her toes.

'Hi,' he said, walking in and depositing the bag on the counter before lifting the two bottles out.

'Hi,' she returned. 'Was everything okay at your mother's?'

His grin widened. 'More than okay. They have the chessboard out. Roger is playing

Sydney and Mom, who are working as a team.'

Jenny chuckled. 'I wonder how that will work out.'

Parker expressed his mirth with an irony that pressed the corners of his lips back. 'I imagine he'll cream them.'

They laughed and chattered as he uncorked the wine, insisting that Jenny taste both the white and the red. Then he exclaimed over the smell of the sauce, growling with hunger.

'Let's eat, woman.'

Jenny let the glass of wine buzz in her head. The spaghetti sauce was delicious, if she did say so herself. It melted in her mouth. She felt sinfully guilty, and tried to ignore the niggling thought that she might live to regret this. But Parker's sensuous gazes over the rim of his glass, the gusto with which he enjoyed the meal and the warmth he didn't try to hide when their fingertips brushed, all uncoiled the bow of desire deep within her.

He helped with the dishes, and they talked about neutral topics: what Sydney was studying in school, what he planned to buy his mother for Christmas. He sought Jenny's advice on the latter, and after starting the coffee to brew, they settled on the couch with some catalogs to browse through.

But the heat between them simmered

before the coffee was ready, and soon Jenny was distracted by fingers massaging the back of her neck.

'Mmmmmm,' she murmured. 'That feels good.'

'Your job makes you tense,' he commented.

'Yes, I suppose.'

'You need to learn to relax.'

Wasn't that what she was doing? 'I guess.'

He reached for the catalog and slowly pulled it out of her hands. Then he wrapped his arms around her and gazed at her lips for a second before he kissed her.

Gone was all inhibition as she kissed him back. They both murmured their pleasure as his hands roamed over her sweater and then found their way to her skin underneath.

'Jenny,' he said with a hoarse sigh, as he nibbled at her earlobe and moved on to her throat.

'What?'

'You make me crazy, you know.'

She giggled a little drunkenly. 'I know.'

They were both crazy, she supposed. Well, wasn't this what everyone had been telling her? That she needed to be a little crazy once in a while? She was glad she'd thought to take care of her diaphragm earlier. When you were having a fling, it was important to be protected.

He leaned her down on the couch, so that his body half covered hers, but left her room to breathe. She was putty in his hands as he took his time dancing his fingers lightly over her skin and then lifted her sweater to gaze raptly at her black lace teddy. His lids were half closed as he tasted each of her mounds with his tongue.

'Do you want me to do this?' he asked her.

'Yes,' she managed to choke out.

'Say it,' he whispered sensuously.

She throbbed with excitement and need that was not untinged with fear. But she knew she had to take this plunge or she'd never get Parker McAllister out of her mind. Little did she know that instead of getting out of her mind, he was simply getting deeper under her skin and into her heart.

'I want you to . . . finish what we started before,' she said huskily.

'I brought protection,' he said.

'It's okay,' she replied, shakily. 'I took care of it.'

Her fingers grasped his thick, dark hair as he began his assault. She felt him loosen the fastening on his tight jeans.

Jenny arched against him as his hands dove under the waistband of her velour leggings. And then he was peeling them off, smiling lazily and lustfully at the extremely high cut of the lace teddy where it angled from above her hips and down to the wisp of lace that passed between her legs to the thong in back.

★   ★   ★

In Dorothy McAllister's apartment, a heated game of chess was underway. Roger had already captured several pawns and a castle and was waiting impatiently for Sydney and Dorothy to make up their minds about their next move.

'Let's move the horse,' said Sydney. 'I like the way he moves.'

She lifted the carved wooden piece and bounced it two squares forward and two to the left.

'No, no, no,' said Roger, rolling his eyes and shoving his glasses back on his nose. 'You can't go that many squares. Here.'

He moved the piece back one square. 'Only two in one direction and *one* to the side.'

'Oh,' said Sydney, unmiffed. 'In that case I want to go this way.'

Roger rested his elbow on the table and drummed the fingers of his left hand on the plastic cloth.

'Well, hurry up, then.'

As if to test his patience, Sydney took her time until she was satisfied that the black horse rested on the square of her choice.

'There,' she said, placing her hands on her hips.

Dorothy nodded. Her chess was elementary, but she enjoyed having her memory refreshed.

'Good move,' she said.

Roger sighed exaggeratedly and contemplated his next move. When he finally decided, he slid his king along one square and rocked back, crossing his arms, a master of strategy.

Sydney and Dorothy stared at the board; then, after much whispering, Sydney moved a pawn forward one square to protect her queen.

Dorothy smiled in satisfaction. 'If you two will excuse me, I need to run across the hall and put my laundry in the dryer. It's my scheduled time, and I have to have it all out in half an hour. Will you two be all right for a few minutes?'

'Sure, Grandma,' answered Sydney.

Roger just screwed up his lips, staring at the board as if to say that he should never have agreed to play this game with girls.

'Then, when I come back, I'll make us some hot chocolate,' said Dorothy cheerily.

The older woman closed the door softly behind her, and Sydney and Roger were left with their game. Roger made his move and then sighed deeply, expecting Sydney to take another half hour to decide what she wanted to do.

But instead, she jumped her horse over a castle and plopped it down in the appropriate square this time. Roger frowned, concentrated, frowned some more. Then he grinned and moved his queen all the way down to sit one square away from her king.

'Check,' he said.

Sydney shrugged, flopping her hands up and then down on her legs. 'You can't do that.'

'Yes, I can. Remember, I told you the queen can move anywhere in a straight line or an angle as long as there's no one in the way.'

'Well, okay, you can have my king. I'd rather have hot chocolate anyway.'

Roger banged her king off the side of the board, making the noise of a dive bomber as the king rolled off the table and bounced onto the carpet.

Sydney tugged at one ponytail. 'We'll win next time.'

Roger shrugged. 'I thought you didn't want to play anymore.'

Sydney tilted her head back and forth, flopping her ponytails. 'We're going to be here for a long time.'

Roger made a face. 'Yeah, I guess so. Too bad we're stuck here. At least at Aunt Jenny's there's a computer. We could play WarCraft. I borrowed it from Grace.'

'Daddy wanted us to stay here.'

Roger squinted his eyes at her. 'Yeah, I guess they like each other.'

He wrinkled his nose in horror at the thought.

But Sydney smiled dreamily. 'I like her. She showed me how to do accounting. Bet you don't know how to do accounting.'

'Do so. I'm a whiz at math.' He sat up proudly and threw back his skinny shoulders.

'I'm going to be an accountant when I grow up,' said Sydney.

'So?'

'So then I can have a job like Jenny's.'

Roger shrugged, as if it didn't matter; then he swept all the chess pieces off onto the tablecloth.

'How long are they going to be over there?' Roger asked, gesturing with his head in the vague direction of Jenny's apartment.

'I don't know,' said Sydney. 'I'm supposed to sleep here.'

Roger made another face. 'Yeah, I heard I get to watch late-night movies here on the couch.'

Then a bright idea lit up his face and he

gave an evil grin. 'We could go spy.'

'How would we do that?' asked Sydney.

Roger rocked his head, thinking, his attitude one of superiority. 'We could climb up to the balcony and hide there.'

Sydney shook her head. 'Too cold. Besides, who cares?'

'Yeah, guess girls don't like to do stuff like that.'

'It's not polite.'

'What's not polite?' he challenged.

'To look.'

'Look at what?' he egged her on.

'My daddy and your Aunt Jenny. I think they want to conjugate.'

11

Jenny lay stretched beneath Parker, still thrilling from their exquisite lovemaking. Even now, as their hearts beat in unison and he cradled his arm around her shoulders, his other hand gently caressed her skin. Their mouths and tongues entangled in an effort to hold on to their intimacy. It had been worth it; these were Jenny's first coherent thoughts.

Worth the risk that she'd get thrown out of her job, worth making herself vulnerable to another man. What was life without this kind of pleasure? Slowly, she settled back to earth, her legs still clinging to his as he moved sideways a few inches to allow her breathing space.

'Wonderful,' he said, nuzzling her ear. 'I thought it would be.'

Wonderful didn't half describe it, and she hated to open her eyes. Though they had left the lights dim, she wanted to remain in her dream. For surely this must be a dream.

He rose to his knees and helped her sit up. The couch wasn't exactly roomy enough for two people to lie beside each other. Embarrassed, now that they had their eyes open, she reached for her clothing.

'Let me do that,' he said.

'It's okay,' she said. 'I need to, um, get dressed before Roger gets back.'

She scooped up her clothing and fled to the bathroom, where she sponged off perspiration and the remains of the evidence. Feeling at once thrilled and uncertain, she returned to the living room to find Parker fully dressed. When their eyes met, she felt that something had changed. But where they would go from here was still a gamble.

'Coffee?' she asked.

'Sounds good.'

She headed for the kitchen, glad for something to do. He followed her. He slid his weight onto the stool and watched her. His droopy eyelids and satisfied smile reminded her of the Cheshire cat. But after she served the coffee and slid onto a stool beside him, he opened his eyes wider.

'That wasn't just a date,' he told her.

'Oh?'

He gave her a direct look. 'I mean, that wasn't just a one-night stand.'

She held her breath, unsure whether she was relieved or frightened. She tried to be nonchalant.

'It's okay. I didn't ask for any promises before we . . . did that.'

'I know.' He reached out and touched her

forearm. 'I just want you to know that I don't do things like that lightly. I want to see you, Jenny.'

'You're seeing me.' She didn't mean to sound so short.

'I want us to get to know each other better.'

'Yeah, okay. Good idea.'

'Jenny, I know you don't trust me. Maybe you don't trust men in general.'

She flinched.

'But you've gotten under my skin. Maybe we can . . . meet halfway.'

Her eyes widened and she stared at him. Then she saw from his apologetic expression that he had phrased that badly.

'No, it's okay,' she said quickly. 'I'm not trying to barge into your life. That conversation with Sydney was . . . accidental.'

He breathed in and out slowly through his nostrils. 'You should know that I've been burned too. Sydney's mother is . . . well, controlling. She wanted a lot. I suppose I want the next woman in my life to accept me for who I am.'

'I can understand that.'

He lifted a corner of his mouth in an ironic smile. 'Do you?'

She held her coffee mug with both hands. 'Everyone wants to be loved for who they are.'

'I could love you, Jenny.'

The admission sent an explosion rocketing from her gut to her ears. Her mug thudded to the countertop, spilling coffee over the side.

'I — don't know what to say,' she said.

He mopped up the spilled coffee. 'Don't say anything until you're ready. We have a lot of things to deal with in our lives. I'm suggesting we take it slow.'

'Uh, yes, slow would be good.'

He reached for her then and turned her so that she leaned back against his chest. His scent filled the space as his arm slid around her waist and under her breasts.

'I'd like to take you home with me,' he said in a lazy, teasing voice.

'What would the neighbors think?' she said, glad to be able to muster a joke when in fact the earth had just moved under her feet.

'What would the spy think?' he teased back in a deep, mock radio announcer voice.

They laughed together, and she regained her own stool. He leaned over and kissed her temple.

'Maybe we'd better go check on those kids of ours.'

'Hmmm. Yes, maybe.'

They put the mugs in the sink and then took their time getting ready to go out. At the door, Parker stopped and pulled her to him again, looking into her face.

'When can I see you again?'

'Anytime. I mean, whenever you're free.'

He gave a regretful smile. 'Until I'm done with the Christmas trees, I'm pretty tied up. I guess I didn't plan to find a beautiful woman at the same time I committed myself to a job with long hours. And I need to finish moving Sydney into the house.'

'I understand.'

He looked pleasantly relieved. 'Good. What about a late supper at my place tomorrow night? Think you can find a baby-sitter?'

Maybe it was all the obstacles they had to overcome to be together that made it a game worth playing. A wild, sensuous weekend with a skilled lover? She would be crazy to say no.

'I'll work on getting a baby-sitter tomorrow.' Her voice was husky.

'Good,' he said, his voice already arousing the new anticipation that raised its head inside her. 'I'll pick you up after the lot closes at eight.'

'I can drive,' she offered. 'It will save time.'

Then she blushed, as if they both knew what they would want to do together as soon as Sydney trundled off to bed.

He considered her offer. 'If you don't mind, maybe that's best. I do have to get Sydney ready for school early Monday morning.'

A little thrill raced through her. He was asking her to spend the night!

'No problem. Just give me directions.'

★   ★   ★

Parker picked up his sleeping daughter and carried her out to the truck. She half woke, but then settled against him, her blanket tucked around her. Her warm trust in him as he drove home filled him with a glow of satisfaction. He was still pleased that she wanted to live with him, and he was willing to turn the world upside down to accommodate that. And the evening's heady lovemaking with Jenny had set him on top of the world.

He gripped the steering wheel harder and concentrated on the road. Better not allow his thoughts to drift in that direction until he could be alone with Jenny again.

Now that he was thinking more seriously about her, he was firming up some plans. They certainly didn't have everything resolved, not by a long shot. But it was clear now that they meant something to each other. He knew Jenny wouldn't take a risk on a man unless she were serious about him. And although he hadn't thought there was room for a woman in his life, now he wanted to make room for Jenny.

He gave Sydney's shoulder a soft squeeze as they pulled into the driveway. Too bad he had to work at the lot tomorrow. Working a job all weekend wasn't the way to lay a foundation for a family life. But that would change soon enough. The Christmas season would be over in another couple of weeks.

★ ★ ★

Jenny allowed the euphoria of Saturday night to carry her through Sunday. Things with Roger were going fairly smoothly when the phone rang. It was Maureen. Just as she'd half expected, arrangements in Maine were taking longer than expected.

'Do you mind having Roger for an extra week?' Maureen begged.

'That's fine,' Jenny said, surprised at how easily agreement came. 'We're doing fine. In fact, I think he sort of wants to play in our big Christmas pageant next weekend. If he's here, that will make it all the easier.'

She could hear her sister's relief. 'That's great. Give him a hug for me, and tell him I promise we'll be home for Christmas.'

'I know you must be exhausted, Maureen,' Jenny said. 'Don't worry about us.'

'You're a chum,' said her sister.

'Thanks.'

Maureen relayed further details about the situation, accepting some of Jenny's advice about what to ask for in the place they had moved John's aunt. Then they hung up.

The rest of the day was spent on household chores, which made the time fly by. When it was time to get ready for another date with Parker, Jenny took a long bubble bath to get in the mood. Roger had found his own baby-sitter. He'd called a friend from the school band, whose mother agreed that he could spend the night. She would get the boys to school tomorrow morning and Jenny would meet the bus after school.

Feeling slightly guilty that she kept having to get rid of Roger in order to see Parker, Jenny hesitated to tell him that his parents wouldn't be back when originally planned. She decided to wait to tell him until tomorrow. Grace would be around then, and the two of them could talk about his part in the Christmas pageant.

All the tasks in her life juggled into place, Jenny fluffed out her hair, sprayed it with a little styling mist, applied the final touches of lipstick and critically checked her appearance. Surely Parker would find her casual look in white leggings, long thick socks and deep blue chenille tunic top fetching for an evening at his home. She didn't forget to pack her diaphragm in her purse. With a tingle of anticipation, she knew how the evening would end. She couldn't spend the night, though. The entire community would see her if she came home in the morning, and their tongues wouldn't be able to wag fast enough.

While driving to Parker's house, she pondered the fact that, after all, even the general manager of a retirement home deserved a social life.

The house was located at the end of a cul-de-sac in a nice residential neighborhood a few miles east of the retirement home. A greenbelt stretched beside the development, now dusted with the light snow they'd accumulated during the week.

When he answered the doorbell, Parker looked even more handsome than he had when she'd seen him last, if that was possible. He swept her against him for a kiss. Laughing, he led her into the spotlessly clean house and showed her around. Sydney dashed down the hall to greet her and showed Jenny her new room, all fixed with her favorite teddy bears and pictures on the walls.

Jenny couldn't remember a more pleasant evening. Parker cooked, and Sydney and Jenny helped. And she shared with both of them some of her plans for the retirement center, careful not to reveal that her ideas could only be implemented if the corporate office felt profits had recovered enough to leave the doors open.

After Parker put Sydney to bed, he returned to the kitchen, where Jenny was washing up. Her nerves jumped a notch or two, and she didn't know what to expect next. Neither one of them had seriously discussed the future, maybe because they both had reasons for avoiding it. But as Parker poured them both another cup of decaf coffee, she noticed the thoughtful look on his face. They carried their coffee to the living room, and she joined him on the brown leather sofa.

He threw one arm over the back of the sofa and gazed at her steadily, making her heart do a little jig. She tried to say something, but the words didn't form. He set his cup down, massaging the back of her neck. But instead of another bout of passion, he seemed in the mood to talk.

'A lot's happened pretty fast,' Parker said. His dark eyes fastened on her face.

'Mmmmm,' she murmured. What did he mean? Was he backpedaling?

'I meant what I said last night,' he told her.

'What?' She wasn't sure what he was referring to.

'I want a serious relationship with you,

Jenny, if that's what you want.'

She swallowed. What *did* she want? She knew in her heart that most of all she wanted him.

'I wasn't, um, expecting anything,' she said. 'I mean, that is . . . '

He grinned. 'I think I know what you mean. What happened last night just happened. But we need to talk about what it means.'

Uh-oh. This didn't sound good, Jenny thought. She tried to give him a noncommittal smile.

'I, uh, know it isn't good to rush things,' she said.

She felt herself flush. She felt like she was being put on the witness stand. She tried to stop feeling so self-conscious and listen to what Parker had to say. It would be better to hear it now than to build pipe dreams on a fantasy foundation.

'Good,' he said. 'I don't want to rush things either. I want to take it nice and slow. I want us to get to know each other better.'

His hands on her neck rubbed harder now, and he was pulling her closer. The heat between them filled her senses, and she had to struggle to keep her hands in her lap. What was the matter with her? Here he was, trying to reduce their flare of uncontrollable passion to logic and a nice period of getting acquainted. But her hormones were aching for attention, for the luscious feelings he could arouse in her. Reckless, but they'd already made love once. Why not again?

Some cautionary fear warned her that the more involved they got, the more it would hurt when they broke up. For, clearly, Parker had his daughter and his job situation to handle. Maybe if they took it slow, things would work out. And what was wrong with that? Hadn't she just told herself that she didn't trust a man with too much else on his mind to want to create a lasting relationship?

But his lips on her collarbone and throat said otherwise. Whatever they were to each other at the moment, they were lovers. She snaked her arms around his neck.

'You're not saying much, Jenny,' he murmured as his lips found her ear.

'How can I?' she breathed.

'Mmmm, guess you're right.' His hands found their way under her tunic top. 'Guess we'll have to talk about this later.'

★ ★ ★

It was nearly midnight when she got home. After a long, warm bath to relax her muscles and indulge in some private thinking time, Jenny asked herself for the hundredth time that week what she thought she was doing. Parker McAllister had swept her away. And they still had not directly confronted the issues facing them. He had a life to get together. And until she saw proof that he was going to take responsibility for himself and his daughter financially, she'd be a fool to get further involved.

She wasn't at all disrespectful of his Christmas job. The man wasn't afraid of hard work. But he'd just lost a position that could have supported a family, and she really didn't know what he would do about that. It would be reckless to set her sights on a man who might prove to be irresponsible. And she didn't know him well enough to know how responsible he was.

He loved his daughter and he was wonderful in bed. He could charm women of all ages, and his mother doted on him. But what did she really know about him?

Jenny closed her eyes and reflected for a delicious moment on what she did know — how his muscles felt under her hands, how he played music on her heart-strings.

She opened her eyes to the bright light again. She splashed around in the bubble bath, trying to think with some sanity about Parker McAllister as a candidate to remain in her love life.

'Ha!' She laughed out loud. Since there wasn't any other competition at the moment, one would think the answer would be easy. But Jenny was still wary. Being hurt once was enough. She didn't want that to happen again.

★   ★   ★

The workweek got underway in a flurry of activity. Grace was in and out of Jenny's office a thousand times, informing her of the latest developments on all the Christmas arrangements. Jenny checked and double-checked supplies for meals for the week, and doubled the cleaning duties to get ready for the inspection team from corporate head-quarters. She proofread her reports carefully, making sure everything was ready for their scrutiny. And of course she thought about the residents, weeding out complaints that were serious from those that simply provided people with something to do with so much time on their hands. The possibility that a major complaint might flare up while the corporate bosses were there was unpleasant.

She and Parker kept in touch by phone. They wouldn't have a chance to see each other until Friday, which was probably a good thing. With the holiday rush, Jenny needed to finish her shopping and mail packages to her folks, and there suddenly seemed to be an endless list of things to do both for Roger and herself.

It wasn't until Wednesday afternoon that Jenny thought to check with Grace about sign-ups for the trip to the art museum on Thursday. Grace was rushing by, her arms full of boxes from the print shop, no doubt containing the printed programs for Saturday's performance. Jenny got up and followed her into her office, a smaller version of Jenny's, with windows on one side only, facing the side lawn.

'Just got the programs,' said Grace, catching her breath. 'Want to look?'

'Sure.'

They slid the tops off the lightweight cardboard boxes and picked up a couple of programs. Grace had requested red and green ink, and the type on the front was shaped like a Christmas tree. Jenny had a momentary qualm about how much the fancy design had cost them, but Grace quickly put her mind at rest.

'I did that in my desktop publishing program on my computer at home. Cute, huh?'

Jenny brightened. She didn't want to comment on her relief that Grace had saved them some money that way. But she thanked her silently.

'That's clever, Grace. Another one of your hidden talents.'

'Oh, I don't hide them that much,' quipped Grace.

Jenny quirked a smile. That was true. Grace wasn't shy about anything, including demonstrating her own abilities.

'Well, it looks great. Is everyone lined up for the dress rehearsal?'

'The players will all be at the staging area at two o'clock.'

'Good. I've let the chef know about all the extra mouths to feed. We'll set up the temporary tables in the commons room for supper that evening.'

Grace beamed her usual enthusiastic smile. 'Excellent.'

Jenny put away the programs, remembering her original reason for coming in here.

'About tomorrow's outing: How many sign-ups do we have?'

Grace pulled a long face. 'Only three, I'm afraid. I was going to check this afternoon. It doesn't seem like the planned outing was a big draw this week.'

'Hmmm,' Jenny replied. 'Maybe it wasn't such a great week to go, with the holidays approaching. But I felt I needed to offer them

262

something in place of the gambling trip I canceled.'

Grace flipped through the clipboard to the copy she'd made of yesterday's sign-up sheet from the front desk. She shook her head.

'It does seem to be unpopular.' She looked up. 'Shall I cancel the van?'

'No,' said Jenny. 'Let's wait until tomorrow morning. If these three want to go to the museum, I'll have Miguel take them.'

'No problem. I'll let Miguel know.'

Miguel was the van driver, who doubled on the maintenance crew.

'Tell him I'll let him know our numbers when he first comes in,' Jenny said. 'That way, he won't have to bring the van around if it's not necessary.'

That task taken care of, Jenny decided she could use a coffee break. It would be time for Roger to get home from school pretty soon.

'How about a cup of coffee?' Jenny suggested.

'Capital idea,' said Grace, following her out of the room.

Carafes of fresh coffee were kept on a sideboard in the commons room. Jenny had had her head buried in paperwork for a solid three days. It was time to relax for a few minutes and take the pulse of the residents.

She and Grace headed out to chat with them for a little while. That way she could watch for Roger to come through the lobby after the bus dropped him on this side of the building.

She visited with a few people on the way, then poured a steaming cup of hot coffee, tempered with milk. Then she carried her cup to the floor-to-ceiling glass windows that looked out over the deck and the garden area. She tried to visualize the plans that Grace had so carefully drawn for Saturday's program. Even though she'd given her approval to every detail, she worried about their extravaganza. A simple indoor program would have been more to her liking.

She let the hot liquid warm her throat as she tried to imagine it. She was glad that Parker would be here to help in case things got a bit disorganized. They might need extra hands at the last minute. She felt a forbidden warmth shoot through her as she thought of the other pleasant tasks his hands could do for her alone. But as Mr. Saito and Mrs. O'Shay's voices broke into her thoughts, she pushed away her personal thoughts and turned to visit with them. She couldn't ignore her residents any longer.

★   ★   ★

Thursday morning, after walking Roger to the bus, Jenny kept her white wool winter coat on and her collar turned up. Snow had been predicted, and already light, moist flakes were beginning to drift down. The three names remained on the sign-up sheet, but neither Grace nor Jenny saw any sign of the residents who'd said they would go to the art museum. Miguel stood with Jenny and Grace by the door in the lobby, awaiting his instructions.

'Bring the van around, Miguel,' Jenny told him. 'They were asked to come down fifteen minutes early, but I don't know where they are.'

'Okay,' said Miguel. He headed toward the back parking lot, where the converted school bus that served as their van was kept.

'Grace, call their rooms. Maybe they forgot.'

Shaking her head, Jenny walked toward her office to shed her coat. Peculiar. Sometimes people were late, but that was why they were asked to be in the lobby twenty minutes early for field trips.

She had just hung up her coat and booted up her computer when Grace came in, looking perplexed.

'Mr. Churchill, Mrs. Callahan and Mrs. Davis aren't in their rooms. I checked the corridors between here and their apartments. They aren't anywhere.'

Jenny frowned. She really didn't need this inconvenience right now. On the other hand, if something dire had happened to any of these people, she needed to know.

'Did you knock on their doors?'

'Yes,' said Grace. She began to look worried. 'Should we take the keys and make sure they're all right?'

'I suppose so. But it would be odd for all three of them to be ill all of a sudden. Go check, anyway. I'll see if they're still in the dining room.'

'They shouldn't be,' said Grace, heading for the desk to get the keys. 'Breakfast was over more than an hour ago.'

Jenny felt a flare of irritation. These three residents weren't senile. They weren't the type to just wander off. She glanced outside as the van chugged around and then idled under the protective awning in the loading area. Then she caught sight of a familiar car parked in a numbered space. She stared at the gray Volvo for a moment before it registered to whom it belonged. The car Parker drove when he didn't have the pickup truck was parked where it shouldn't be.

She exhaled a breath of exasperation. Why was he parked in a staff parking area? He

266

should know he was supposed to park in visitor parking. She felt a twinge of annoyance that she would have to mention it to him. She also wondered why he was visiting his mother at this hour. Usually he went straight to the tree lot after dropping Sydney off at school.

Miguel left the motor running to warm it up and stepped out of the van. When he came in, she shook her head.

'We're checking their units, Miguel. Sorry. I guess you'll have to wait a few minutes.'

'No problem.'

Confused about what was going on, Jenny walked purposefully toward the corridor to the units. She would find Grace and see if she'd learned anything.

On the second floor, she caught up with Grace and the head housekeeper outside the open door of Mr. Churchill's apartment. The other woman shook her head as she locked the door again.

'He's not here. Nothing seems to be amiss. I wonder where he's gone.'

Jenny sighed, resting a fist on her hip. 'You'd think they would have let the desk know they'd changed their plans. What about the others?'

Grace lifted her hands in a broad gesture of perplexity. 'Not home.'

For the second time, irritation flared in Jenny. Just how much time should they dedicate to finding out what had happened to them? Technically, it was the residents' own responsibility to sign the book at the desk whenever they left the grounds. But no one had signed out.

'Well, I guess we'd better check the basement.'

Grace followed her to the elevator, frowning in puzzlement. 'The beauty shop's not open yet, and there's no exercise class down there this morning.'

The clock was ticking in Jenny's mind. She really needed to get back to her desk. There were still a myriad of things to do before the corporate team arrived at noon. She realized how tightly she was wound. She had even dressed in her best tweed suit and ivory silk blouse. The future of the establishment as well as her own job depended on what happened here in the next few days. Missing residents was not part of the picture.

As soon as the elevator doors opened at the basement level, Jenny and Grace looked at each other. Voices raised in a clamor came to them from down the hall.

'Must be in the rec room,' Grace muttered.

They stalked along the hallway until they came to the turn. Low wooden planters

268

delineated the large tiled room used for exercise sessions. But the sight they confronted was so astonishing, Jenny dropped her mouth open.

Card tables had been set up, filled with residents, four to a table. They bent over small, colored cards filled with large, easy-to-read numbers. Round, plastic disks were piled beside the players. But what stunned Jenny the most was that Parker stood at the head of the room, spinning a wire cage full of wooden balls. Dressed in a navy blue button-down oxford shirt and fawn-colored corduroy trousers, he whirled the handle, let go and then picked up the wooden ball that dropped into the tray.

'B thirteen,' he called out, obviously enjoying himself.

A murmur swelled from those who had the number, who excitedly placed markers on their cards.

Parker smiled at the crowd and spun the handle again.

'Good Lord,' said Grace, halted beside her. 'A bingo game.'

Jenny shut her mouth. The missing residents were there, all three of them enjoying themselves, obviously giving no thought to the fact that they'd held up the van and caused a great deal of concern.

Jenny's indignation boiled. She saw Dorothy McAllister in the crowd.

'Grace,' she hissed. 'This wasn't on the schedule, was it?'

'No,' said Grace, dismayed and wringing her hands. 'Of course not.'

'Inveterate gamblers,' Jenny grumbled through clenched teeth. 'The least they could have done was tell us.'

'I'm surprised Parker didn't mention it,' Grace said.

Jenny felt a stab of anger. 'Well, he didn't.'

She turned on her heel and stalked back to the elevator. She couldn't fume in front of all of them. Just how she would handle this demonstration of rebelliousness, she wasn't in the frame of mind to decide right then. And she wasn't in any mood to talk to Parker, either.

Grace hurried after her, catching up just as the elevator doors opened. The program director saw Jenny's black mood and pinched her lips together. Once they emerged on the first floor, Grace rushed along, keeping up with Jenny's furious pace.

'Shall I tell Miguel to put away the van?' she asked.

'Yes,' snapped Jenny. 'Tell him there won't be any more *cultural* outings this week.'

12

Parker had seen Jenny's murderous look from where she and Grace stood behind the planter. He called the next number, then glanced Jenny's way again. His jovial smile died on his lips when he saw the fury in her eyes. But what the matter was, he couldn't guess.

Round and round went the handle on the cage.

'Give us an O seventy-five,' one of the elderly gents called.

Everyone laughed, and then quavering voices began to holler out the numbers they wanted. He glanced at his mother, who was serenely placing her marker on the number he'd just called.

He picked up the wooden ball. 'I seventeen,' he said.

Again his gaze flew to Jenny, who had darts in her eyes. Then he watched her turn on her heel and stomp off. Clearly she wasn't pleased about this bingo game, but he couldn't imagine why. Grace caught his eye for a moment before, looking bewildered, she followed Jenny away.

Trepidation slithered down his spine. It had slipped his mind to mention the game to Jenny. After all, when they were together, they had other things on their minds. He assumed his mother had taken care of the details here at the home. After all, it had been at Dorothy's request that he'd come today and run their game. Hadn't Jenny known about it? More dread seethed in his gut. He was in trouble, that was for sure.

He pushed the worry aside and called out more numbers until someone called, 'Bingo!'

Then they shuffled cards and markers as he began another round. He wouldn't be out of here for another hour. He knew the stress must be getting to Jenny this week. He thought he remembered her saying that the corporate team arrived today. Oh, damn! Could that be it? If his mother had conned him into running a bingo game that hadn't been cleared with management, it might be awkward, even disastrous, for Jenny. But what was the harm in a little bingo game? They were only playing for pennies.

He tried to keep a pleasant smile on his face as he called out more numbers. He narrowed his eyes at his mother, unable to speak to her privately right now. Dorothy smiled contentedly, as if nothing was wrong. Puzzled, Parker continued with the game.

* ★ ★

Emerging from the corridor, Jenny stopped suddenly, reaching out to grasp Grace's arm, bringing her to a sudden halt near the Christmas tree.

'What?' said Grace. Her fingers pried at Jenny's, trying to undo the viselike grip.

Jenny softly swore an oath that made Grace's eyes open wide. Jenny rarely swore, and never like a sailor in a brothel. She followed Jenny's shocked gaze to the desk, where two men and a woman in dark business suits were just shedding their coats. The briefcases on the floor were an additional clue.

'Uh-oh,' said Grace. 'I thought they weren't coming until later.'

'So did I,' said Jenny, the tension in her voice sounding even more stressed than before.

'What do we do?'

Jenny drew in a deep breath and sighed. 'Nothing to do but greet them.'

She took a step forward and then grabbed Grace's arm again.

'Wait!'

'What?' Grace said again.

Jenny gave her a wide-eyed look of horror. 'The bingo game.'

'Ohhhhh,' said Grace. 'You want to keep them away.'

Jenny's jaw clenched and unclenched. 'They'll read the schedule and see we had a trip to the art museum planned. If they see the game in progress instead, they'll think I planned badly.'

Grace thought Jenny was overreacting, but she wanted to pitch in and help her boss stay out of hot water.

'We can say the bus broke down.'

'No, no,' said Jenny. 'We can't start lying; we'd only get trapped in the lies eventually. Damn. I'll try to keep them up here for an hour. You go downstairs and try to move that blasted game somewhere else. Whisper in Parker's ear that the corporate team is here and will be doing their inspection. I can't risk them seeing a bingo game.'

Grace raised an eyebrow. 'Nor can we risk a volume of resident complaints while they're here.'

Jenny's face grew black with resentment. 'It's Parker's fault. He's not going to hear the end of this. Go do what you can.'

Then she smoothed her tweed skirt, plastered a professional smile on her face and walked forward to greet the team from headquarters. Under her breath, she was cursing Parker for going behind her back and for disastrous timing.

'Oh, damn,' she whispered, just before her heels touched the tiled lobby floor. Parker's car was still in staff parking. If they thought a staff member drove a Volvo, they might think she was paying the staff something on the side. Or worse.

'Mr. Redlin,' she said to the tall gentleman with curly gray hair ringing a balding crown. The CEO of Cherry Valley Retirement Homes, International, Charles Redlin was a smooth talker, but from what Jenny had seen at her interview and from subsequent correspondence, she knew that Charlie, as the company referred to him, could be tough as nails.

'Ms. Knight,' he said, his blue eyes beaming as he turned around for a formal handshake. 'How nice to see you again. I'm sorry if our early arrival is going to cause you any inconvenience. We were able to make an earlier flight because of a last-minute meeting cancellation.'

I'll bet, thought Jenny. They probably knew all along they were going to get here early, hoping to surprise the staff.

'Not at all,' she said with a bright smile as he continued to pump her hand. 'We're very glad to welcome you at any time.'

'Let me introduce Sherryl MacIntyre,

vice-president of marketing.'

The extremely well made-up woman in chic gray checks reached out her hand. Her short dark hair was styled over her ears with long wisps at the back of the neck. Jenny took her hand carefully to avoid impaling herself on the woman's long red nails.

'Nice to meet you, Ms. MacIntyre,' said Jenny, her smile glued in place.

'A great pleasure, Ms. Knight,' said the marketing VP. 'I've heard you're doing a fabulous job with this place.'

'I hope so,' returned Jenny.

The other man was introduced as Mr. Aoki. He was a square-built Asian with solid shoulders and a rock-hard handshake that put her in mind of a martial arts devotee. He gave a little bow as he shook hands with her.

'Pleased to meet you, Ms. Knight.' He had a slight Japanese accent, but his English was fluent.

With a sinking heart, Jenny wondered suddenly if the parent company was planning to sell her grandmother's old home to a foreign interest. She knew the Japanese often had their own way of running businesses and doubted that kind of change would work in this cock-eyed, rambling place.

'Thank you,' said Jenny. 'Would you all like a cup of coffee or tea? If you'd like to freshen up after your flight, I can show you where the rest rooms are.'

'Thank you,' said Charlie, 'but I think we might like to stretch our legs first. Sitting on the plane and then driving the rental car here didn't do anything for our backs. I had to give up my morning racquetball game to make the flight.'

They all laughed pleasantly as Jenny fought the knot in her stomach.

'Of course,' said Jenny, thinking madly. What they wanted was a tour. *Now*. She smiled sweetly. 'Then why don't you leave your briefcases in my office, and we'll begin our tour.'

If they wanted to play hardball, so could she. But she would make damn sure they kept out of the basement recreation room until Grace got that bingo game out of there. She knew without a doubt that these three keen-eyed executives wouldn't miss a thing. And to let them know that the residents had openly rebelled against her program plans and roped a resident's son into running an unannounced game where gambling was taking place would put Jenny's neck on the line.

After a five-minute rest-room break, they regrouped in Jenny's office, where she quickly laid out her professionally formatted reports on the conference table. Maybe she could buy time by distracting them with the reading material. But after a swift glance and some compliments, they all stood there like a platoon ready to march.

'Let's begin in the kitchen, if you don't mind,' said Jenny. 'We're just between breakfast cleanup and lunch preparations. If we go in now, we won't be in the chef's way.'

They followed her agreeably, making small talk as they went. Jenny led them through the spotlessly clean kitchen. She began to feel rewarded for her efforts this week as they made approving remarks. Charlie asked some intelligent questions of the chef, who, though he eyed them all suspiciously, swung open freezer doors and produced the dietitian's recipes he followed. The chic Ms. MacIntyre gushed over the arrangements, and Jenny began to feel some hope.

Then she marched them through the newly renovated lobby and pointed out all the features that had shown up on the endless itemized budgets and final reports. She managed to kill a half hour on the main floor, thanking her lucky stars every time they had to pause to let a slower-moving elderly resident cross their path. Then she took them to the top floor to work their way down to the lobby again. By the time they had inspected the scrupulously organized supply closets and several laundry rooms on each floor, there was nothing left to do but the basement.

Back in the parlor again, Mr. Aoki consulted a layout in his leather portfolio.

'The exercise room,' he said. 'Where is it?'

'Uh, it's in the basement. I think there might be a class in there right now.'

'No problem,' said Mr. Aoki. 'We just want to see the exercise equipment.'

Jenny raised a hand to stop him, but he pivoted and walked toward the staircase that led downward to the library. She followed him on wobbly knees trying to drum up an explanation in her mind as she went. The other two followed her, and they threaded their way through the library and into the corridor. Two elderly residents ambled past, leaning on their walkers. Mr. Aoki bowed.

As they took the next few steps, Jenny saw a flicker of movement at the far end of the hall. She thought she saw the flash of Grace's skirt disappearing around the corner.

To Jenny's immense relief, there was no one in the exercise room. The card tables were bare. That was a close call!

'Ah, the exercise mats,' exclaimed Mr. Aoki as he marched over to pinch them. He gave a grunt of approval. 'Good quality.'

He checked something off on his list, and

for the moment Jenny couldn't be bothered to worry about whether it was good or bad. She realized her pulse was still pounding, but, thankfully, everything down here appeared just as it should.

'Well,' she said, relieved that the tour was over now, 'shall we go up to my office?'

★   ★   ★

Lunch was followed by their business meeting, during which Jenny answered every question the executives fired at her. Grace joined them for part of the meeting, giving Jenny some respite from being on trial. But she had to keep an eye on Grace, too, to make sure that her exuberance didn't lead her to say something the others might not appreciate. But to her credit, Grace was charming and professional. By the end of the meeting, she and Charlie were sharing jokes like old friends. Good thing Grace could be so relaxed, thought Jenny as she stole glances at the clock, waiting for the ordeal to be over.

She was also glad they didn't invite her to dinner that evening. One more minute in their presence would just be too much. She'd made it plain that she was taking care of her nephew, so they must have gotten the message that she wasn't available. When she saw them off in their rental car late that afternoon, it wasn't a minute too soon.

'Quite a day,' said Grace, who came out to the lobby when Jenny returned. Grace brushed her hands together, as if satisfied with a job well done.

Jenny sagged in relief. 'All I want now is a glass of wine and a hot bath.'

'Sounds like a good idea to me,' agreed Grace.

'By the way, where did you scoot that bingo game off to this morning?' she asked.

Grace grinned. 'I told McAllister that we were under siege. They went to the community hall in the apartment complex across the street. I'm friendly with management there and told them we were in a bind.'

Amazing Grace! 'You're a lifesaver,' Jenny told her.

'Not a problem.'

They bid each other so long, and then Jenny trudged along to her apartment. Roger had gone home with a friend after school, so she would be able to unwind by herself. Thoughts of Parker gnawed at her, but there wasn't any way to call him at the tree lot. There wasn't a phone in the temporary trailer office. When she next saw him, though, she was going to give the man a piece of her mind.

A knock sounded on the door just as she was finally dragging herself out of the bathtub. She went to answer it, her blue terry-cloth robe the only thing covering her damp body, and her hair pinned up out of the way.

'Who is it?'

'It's me, Jenny,' came Parker's familiar voice.

She opened the door before she realized she was only half dressed. Then she stepped behind it as he entered.

'Hi there,' he said with a grin, shutting the door and sliding his arms around her waist.

Annoyance and anger pricked, even as the feel of his muscular body against hers set off a different response. She pulled away.

'If you'll wait a minute, I'll put on some clothes.'

'I don't want you to put on any clothes,' he said, reaching for her again, his mouth aiming for hers.

But her hands on his shoulders slowed him down. He stopped his advances immediately.

'We have some things to talk about,' she told him. 'Wait until I've changed.'

'Jenny,' he said, still trying to attack from the flank, 'I think I figured out that there was a misunderstanding this morning. I've come to make up for it.'

'Hmmm,' she huffed. But this time she didn't push him away. 'That's an understatement,' she said.

She wasn't about to let him sweet-talk his way out of this without a thorough lecture. There were some things he needed to understand about how she ran her business. But in the meantime, his hands were already working their magic, and she was having trouble with the crazy desire that was spiraling through her. His fingers were creeping under the edges of the robe and peeling it back. His mouth found hers and his lips nibbled hers.

'I missed you,' he said. 'And I can explain everything.'

A crazy desire to have sex first and talk later swelled within her. But she fought it.

'Where's Roger?' he asked, reminding her that their rare privacy would only last until nine o'clock, the curfew she'd felt she needed to impose on a school night.

'He's over at a friend's house. But Parker, I have to talk to you.'

'Hmmmm,' he said, nuzzling her throat while his hands stroked her hip and roamed around toward her thighs. 'I know.'

'Parker . . . ' She made one more try, dizzy already at the effects his hands and tender kisses had on her sensitive skin.

'Yes, Jenny?'

'You . . . ' She swallowed, shivering at what he was doing to her nether regions.

'I what?'

He shifted her to the couch. There, he laid her down and untied her robe so he could gaze lovingly at the tantalizing sight of her.

'You can't park in a numbered parking spot,' she said as if from a great distance as he made quick work of his belt and pulled off his polo shirt.

His gaze met hers unflinchingly as he unzipped his trousers and slid them off. Then he scooped her into his arms as he climbed onto the couch, covering her with his body.

'I'll keep that in mind,' he said as his head came close to hers and he took her lips in a breathtaking kiss.

Then she didn't resist anymore. Her quivering body reached out for his, and she let the relaxation she had achieved in the warm bath climax in this delicious, sensuous experience. Nothing was settled, she reminded herself before Parker carried her off to ecstasy. But her body seemed to want what he was offering more than she could organize her thoughts.

'Mmmmm,' she murmured as he kissed her in very private places and slid up to warm her. 'Talk later.'

'Much later,' he whispered.

When they sprawled breathless some time later, Jenny realized that she could fall asleep. After her tense day, being in Parker's arms was heaven. But all wonderful things had to end, and Roger was due home in a short time.

'Have to rouse ourselves,' she muttered, as if she was drunk. But she hadn't had any more wine than the one glass after work.

He lifted his head from her breast and bored his Cheshire cat gaze into her eyes.

'Now, what were you saying about a parking place?'

Jenny pulled herself up and gathered her robe around her.

'Why don't you make us some coffee and I'll go change?' She staggered off to the bedroom to find her clothes and her thinking process.

★ ★ ★

They talked it out. Jenny vented, but then accepted Parker's explanation of what had happened. He shook his head sorrowfully.

'Mom asked me to do this last week. I assumed she'd cleared it with someone.'

His big shoulders shrugged, and Jenny's roiling emotions settled down enough to allow her to believe him.

'I guess I was being sent a signal by the residents,' she said. 'I just wish they'd come to me to talk it over first.'

'Yeah, people do that to you sometimes.'

She felt herself drowning in his concerned gaze. She wasn't going to hold a grudge. There was no point.

'Why did you leave your car in the numbered parking?' she finally asked, just wanting to finish crossing every *t*.

She could tell he was trying not to be amused, and she didn't know whether she should be angry or not. He did seem as if he was trying to make amends.

'I was in a hurry,' he said. 'I had all that stuff to carry in. I didn't think I'd be there very long. And I really didn't think it mattered.'

'It matters,' she said, the stress of the day still a weight. 'Mostly because the big guns might question it.'

'Sorry. I'll make sure to use visitor parking after this.'

She knew what they were discussing was trivial, but it was another indication of how they each operated. She did things by the rules; Parker, she was beginning to see, glowed things right. He must believe in himself so much that he just assumed everything would work out. Did she want a man who didn't always play fair?

'Jenny, Jenny' he said, wrapping his arms around her. 'I want to make things right for you. You'll see.'

He kissed her temple and her forehead in a comforting gesture rather than a passionate one.

'Hmmmm,' she mumbled into his sweater.

'I promise I'll park wherever you say from now on,' he told her.

'Well, okay,' she said.

He held her and comforted her, and then they spoke of other things. Before he left, they opened the French doors and went out onto her balcony. The frosty night was bright with snow on the ground, but the sky had cleared and pinpoints of stars were visible. Parker held her in front of him as they looked out at the stars.

'Make a wish upon a star?' he murmured into her ear.

'That would be nice,' she mused. Then she gave a deep sigh. 'I guess I wish I had a star of my own to retreat to when I needed to.'

'Hmmmm. Jenny's star.'

She nodded. 'A fantasy getaway place, you know, with magic and waterfalls and lush forests.'

'Oh, an ideal world. Can I come?'

'Maybe.'

He nuzzled her neck and tightened his hold on her. 'I'm only getting you your own star if I can come.'

'All right,' she said, finally able to let loose and be playful. 'You can come. And . . . '

She turned around in his arms, feeling normal for the first time all day.

'And what?' he asked. 'I need to know what you want me to get you for Christmas.'

'Oh,' she teased him, 'a star will be enough.'

A secret grin lit his face. 'Nothing else?'

'Well,' she said, letting a thought surface that had been buried since last summer. It made little sense, but it popped up right then and there in her mind. 'I'd like a puppy.'

His eyes came alert. 'Are you serious?'

'Why not? After Roger leaves, there won't be anyone else in the apartment but me. I've gotten used to the company. I've thought of getting a puppy for companionship.'

His smile was sly. 'You're forgetting that I intend to provide you with companionship.'

'I know,' she said seriously, lifting her hand to trace his face. 'But we're still in the getting-to-know-you-stage, aren't we?'

One of his dark eyebrows lifted as he studied her face. But she bested him with her own teasing.

'I can train a puppy.'

He gave a growl and lifted her up off her feet, spinning her around and setting her back down inside the French doors.

'I guess that means I'm untrainable.'

Jenny really didn't want to discuss the matter any further, and the time had passed for discussions. They dimmed all the lights except the ones on the Christmas tree and stretched out before her fireplace, sharing an intimacy that would heal all wounds and get them through all the seemingly unsurmountable obstacles.

'I love you, Jenny,' he said when they were stretched out before a flickering fire.

'Hmmm, love,' she responded lazily.

She wasn't sure if that was her declaration, or if it was still too soon for her to commit her feelings to him. What would it take? she wondered as she almost dozed in the warmth of his arms. Could they be together for the rest of their lives? Was this going to work?

'I promise I'll get you a puppy,' he whispered into her ear as his fingers tickled her skin under her sweater.

'I promise Jenny Knight a puppy and a star of her very own.'

13

On Friday, the corporate inspection team ate their way through three meals in the dining room, complimenting the food and appearing satisfied with the service. Jenny never sat down. Instead, she greeted the residents and kept an eye on the wait staff, ready to pounce if there were any problems.

In between trips to the dining room, Charlie, Mr. Aoki and Sherryl MacIntyre quizzed the head housekeeper, observed the nurses' aides doing their jobs, followed maintenance men about as they did repairs and met twice in Jenny's office to discuss the imminent price hike. Jenny produced surveys of what other retirement homes in similar locales were charging. Costs were going up. Jenny just worried that the rent increase might be a hardship on some of her residents.

But the three executives kept poker faces, neither discouraging her nor encouraging her. Then Charlie dropped his bombshell.

'By the way, Jenny, we've decided to stay until Sunday, if you don't mind putting up with us for one more day.'

'Oh?' Jenny felt her blood drain away but

kept her face neutral.

'Airline tickets cheaper if we stay over Saturday night,' Mr. Aoki informed her.

Of course Jenny knew that. She pressed her lips together, knowing full well that they had probably planned this a long time ago. They had told her they would only be here for two days. The weekend hadn't been part of the deal. Well, obviously it was now. She was forced to mention tomorrow's Christmas production, since they'd be here in the thick of it.

'We will start setting up in the morning,' she told them. 'There will be a rehearsal early in the afternoon so that all the groups participating know their parts. Grace has, um, done an excellent job in orchestrating the whole program.'

Sherryl looked over the red and green printed programs.

'Charming,' she said. Her expression didn't relay any emotion at all. 'I'm sure we'll enjoy it.'

And judge just how organized or not this place is, Jenny wanted to say, but didn't. She sat down at her desk.

'I hope so,' she finally said. 'The residents are looking forward to it.'

Were they? Oh, Lord. Another day to seal her fate. She closed her eyes and opened them again. How would she live through one more day of scrutiny from these people? And all the while balance her personal life.

Charlie stood up and tossed the last of the reports on the table.

'Well, we've all worked hard today. I say we take the evening off. I'm anxious to visit the gym recommended by the hotel before dinner. Ms. Knight, would you care to accompany us to the Fort for dinner? I've heard dining in the mountains is a must-do when one comes to visit your fair city.'

'Thank you, but my nephew . . . '

'Oh, of course. I'd forgotten. I understand that family must come first.' He let her off the hook. 'We'll be seeing you tomorrow anyway.'

She rose and escorted them all to the door. 'Yes, that's true. But I'm sure you'll enjoy the Fort. You must try the wild game.'

'I intend to,' said Charlie as they all got into their coats.

She saw them off and then went into Grace's office to collapse into a chair and take off her shoes. Grace eyed her over the paper she was reading.

'Summit over?'

Jenny shook her head wearily. 'No. I'm afraid they've decided to stay over until Sunday. At least they just now decided to tell me of that decision. You'll have to reserve them front-row seats for tomorrow's program.'

Grace rolled her eyes. 'Well, so the VIPs need to be entertained.'

'I'm not sure entertained is the right word,' Jenny said in a wry tone. 'But we can't roll up the red carpet yet.'

Grace waved an arm. 'So much the better, then. I'll encourage all of my troupe by telling them that they will be playing to a very important house. It will inspire them.'

'I hope it will inspire them and not terrify them.'

Grace gave her a sympathetic look. 'I very much doubt that the people performing in tomorrow's Christmas extravaganza are the sort to be terrified.'

'Let's just hope all goes well and we avoid terrifying anybody.'

Grace gave her a sharp salute. 'Not a problem. I guarantee that the production will be memorable.'

Later, at home, Jenny fell asleep on the couch. When Parker called after he got off work, she was too exhausted to be coherent on the phone. Though she wanted to see him, she was somewhat relieved that they hadn't planned to be together that night. She needed a good night's rest.

'I'll see you tomorrow afternoon,' he said in

a reassuring tone. 'The kids are all ready for the program. Don't worry. I'll help with the supervision and make sure none of them get cranky.'

The memory of the sock in the tuba came to mind, but she was too tired to worry about anything more that evening.

'I'm glad you'll be here,' she told him frankly. 'I have a feeling we'll need your help.'

He spoke some tender words that warmed her heart, and then they hung up. After seeing Roger off to bed, she turned in. A full moon showed out the French doors of her bedroom, and Jenny remembered Parker's fanciful promise of last night. For a moment she let herself imagine flying away with him on a magic carpet to their own private star. And what should she get him for Christmas?

★   ★   ★

The inspection team didn't show up at the retirement home until noon on Saturday, which gave Jenny some breathing space. She left the program setup in Grace's capable hands but kept an eye out for any oversights. All the deliveries occurred on time, and she conferred with Grace about seating arrangements and went over the rehearsal schedule once more.

Just before the rehearsal, Jenny glanced out of her windows to see the Volvo pull up with Parker and Sydney inside. Her heart warmed, and a flood of emotional relief filled her. In spite of all her doubts about Parker's level of responsibility, instinct told her that she needed to lean on him today. And wasn't that what she wanted? Someone she knew instinctively was going to be there for her? She couldn't exactly pin it on logic, but a swelling inside her said she could depend on him. She plucked a tissue from its box, needing to blot her eyes from the sudden emotion. She knew she was stressed beyond belief, and that the holiday season on top of a new relationship was making her less than logical. But there would be time to analyze all this later.

Moments later, Parker strode into her office, and it was all she could do to keep herself from throwing herself into his arms. But with Sydney present and the door open, she stood and kept her fingers on the desk surface, greeting him with a shaky smile.

He, however, had no such inhibitions and came around the desk to drop a kiss on her lips. It warmed her that he was willing to demonstrate his affection for her in front of Sydney.

'Hope we're in time,' he said.

She nodded, wanting to hold on to him longer. She actually felt teary, she was so glad to see him. She bent and gave Sydney a hug.

'I'm glad to see both of you. I guess Grace is ready to direct the rehearsal.'

Parker gave her a broad grin. 'Shall we?'

The trailers with the animals had pulled around in back, and they found Grace outside, directing the unloading. Portable pens had been set up in the space behind the building, close to the plaza where the stage was now set up. Parker went to help Hank DeVere set up risers for the kids on the ground at stage left. As the children began to arrive, shrieks went up and they surrounded the trainer leading a reddish-brown, two-humped camel down a ramp. But Grace was prepared.

'Now, now, children. Stay back. The camel is going into the pen over here. One at a time can come up to the fence and pet him when the trainer says so.'

A few feet from the camel pen, some sheep were being herded into their own pen by a man in a soft tweed cap.

Jenny closed her eyes, wondering if the corporate office was going to appreciate the apparent petting zoo. Of course, the home had dogs and cats brought in to visit with the residents. It had been proven that petting animals was good for morale and health. But this was a little beyond that. Not only children but some residents began to drift over to see the animals. But the adults kept respectfully back. Jenny decided she'd better go find Charlie and his team and explain.

As she hurried up the stairs from the lower-level library to the lobby, she saw Mr. Mossback's large frame disappearing down the hall toward her office.

Wondering what he wanted, she crossed the lobby and stepped into the hallway just in time to see him turning around. In his hand was a piece of paper. Behind him the fax machine beeped.

'Mr. Mossback, do you need something?'

He shoved the paper behind his back and shook his head quickly. 'No, no. Nothing. I . . .'

He turned to glare at the fax machine behind him. 'This thing was making noise. Sounded like my son's machine when it's out of paper.'

Jenny frowned. Something was fishy here. She had clearly caught him doing something he didn't want found out.

'Oh, is it out of paper?'

She stepped forward. Then she reached out and snatched the piece of paper he was trying to hide behind his back.

'Here, I can fax this for you, if you like. There's more paper in my office.'

Then she looked down at the paper. She would never have read the private correspondence of one of her residents, but the name at the top of the paper confirmed her suspicions. He was sending a fax to Mabel, the executive secretary at corporate headquarters. She was Jenny's contact for sending in reports, and a gossip who seemed to know everything before Jenny could tell her.

She looked up at Mr. Mossback, who seemed to be having trouble meeting her gaze.

'Mr. Mossback, I didn't know you knew Mabel.'

He was a big man, but she'd cornered him, and his big shoulders slumped. His eyes glanced furtively past her, as if he was seeking a way out. But Jenny wasn't about to be outsmarted.

'Would you like to come sit in my office and tell me about this?'

Like a guilty schoolboy, he went in the way she pointed. She offered him a chair, into which he squeezed his large girth. Then she closed the door. She still hadn't let go of the paper in her hand.

'Have you been faxing information about the retirement home to Mabel?'

He stuck out a lower lip. 'My business,' he said.

'My business, I think,' said Jenny, still standing in front of him. Then she circled her desk.

'I thought Mabel had a friend here. Someone who was anxious to provide the corporate office with information before I could.'

He frowned at the floor but didn't say anything. She knew she couldn't discipline him in any way; she had to maintain good relations. But she was going to find out why he was doing this if it was the last thing she did on this job.

'Why?' she asked him simply. 'Is there a reason?'

She waited a long time. But a silent listener invites speech, and finally he snuck a look at her.

'Mabel is my friend.'

'I can see that. How did she become your friend?'

He made an awkward wave of his hand. 'Long time ago. During the war.'

'Oh?' He must be speaking about World War II. 'How did you meet?'

'Overseas. It was classified business at the time.'

Jenny blinked and sat down. Something

299

about this story was more unusual than she'd expected. And she could tell by the way he hesitated that it must be the truth.

'You met Mabel when you were in the service? But she must have been a child.'

He nodded several times. 'She was ten. Her parents were in my spy ring.'

'You were a spy, Mr. Mossback? This is fascinating. I've been wanting to learn more of the history of the residents here. I had hoped we could write up some of these stories. But what does this have to do with your feeding her information about this place?'

He shrugged. 'When I found out that little Mabel was working for the corporate office, we sent messages back and forth. It sort of felt like the old days.'

He folded his hands between his knees, looking down again. Jenny was beginning to get the picture.

'So you just fell into your old habits, giving her useful information.'

'She seemed to like it.'

'I'll bet she did.'

Jenny leaned back in her chair. She had caught her spy, all right. Now what should she do?

She spoke more gently now. 'Well, you don't need to send her secret reports now,

Mr. Mossback. Her bosses are here in person to gather information.'

He nodded. 'I know.'

Was there something else? Something she was missing? She observed him carefully.

'Have you seen Mabel recently?'

A tinge of color passed over his wrinkled face. 'Ten years ago. She came out here. That's when we ran into each other. We had quite a time, reminiscing about the old days.'

He was smitten with the woman! Jenny's eyes widened, but she didn't say anything. It all fit together. Mr. Mossback had a crush on Mabel and was feeding her information like a schoolboy, to gain approval. It would have been quaint had it not been at her expense.

'I see,' she said. 'Well, I'm glad you've told me all this, Mr. Mossback.'

She even found herself able to grin a little at the situation. What more unlikely thing could possibly occur at Cherry Valley Retirement Home this season? They'd already had a romance, children fighting, stolen supply carts, a sock in a tuba, and an illicit bingo game.

'May I read your fax now?' she asked him.

'I guess so.'

Sure enough, it was a note to Mabel, informing her that livestock was being unloaded right at this moment. He described the preparations for the Christmas program. But at the end of the note, she saw his sentimental touch.

'Wish you could see it, Mabel. It should prove to be quite a spectacle.'

Jenny's eyes moistened. This was nothing but an old man hanging on to a touching relationship and remembering the thrill of his youth. She handed the note back.

'You can go ahead and send it to her now, if you like. I'll get the extra paper.'

Her anger disappeared as she refilled the fax machine. Then she touched Mr. Mossback on the arm and walked away, leaving him to play spy with a woman he had held close to his heart for a long time.

★ ★ ★

Jenny sat with the corporate team inside the library, where they could look out the glass windows at what was going on outside. But she ceased worrying about every detail. She kept her eyes on Parker, who stood on the sidelines, watching the program go through its paces. He moved chairs for the elderly readers who needed to get up to the podium. He joked with his mother, and he went dashing off to hoist lights and test electrical plug-ins when needed.

Jenny began to care less about the three number crunchers next to her and more about how much the residents and the volunteers were enjoying themselves. After all, wasn't that what life was all about? And Mr. Mossback, living out his fantasy. Jenny was beginning to believe that she was doing a good job here, and if her bosses couldn't see that, then it would be their shortsightedness and not her fault for lack of trying. She sat silently, just letting them watch until they decided to take a break and stretch their legs.

But Jenny sat there by herself for a long time, realizing that she wasn't needed. Grace had planned everything out well, and the volunteers were proud of their contributions. Hank DeVere kept the kids under control, and Roger and the choir's accompanist seemed to be working well together. What did Jenny have to worry about?

By the time she drifted upstairs for a cup of coffee, she found herself looking forward with immense enthusiasm to the dinner break. She wanted to see Parker stride across the parlor toward her again. She wanted to see that look of love on his face. Oh, she had so much to tell him now. Now that she trusted him to take care of things.

At the dinner break, Parker did stride across to her, finding her by the Christmas tree. But they barely had time to smile at each other before being interrupted by the hubbub of the occasion. Suddenly there seemed to be fifty people to talk to. Parents, residents, volunteers, staff, all seemed in a flurry. Jenny helped direct some of the guests into the commons room, where additional tables had been set up. Then she helped the wait staff by pouring coffee herself and assisting when residents needed something.

From the other side of the room, she saw Parker performing a similar role with the choir kids and his mother's coffee klatch. They would have their chance to be together later.

The opportunity came when everyone else was eating. Parker made his way through the crowd and slid an arm around her waist.

'Got a minute?'

She smiled up at him. 'I think I can break away for a few minutes. Why?'

A twinkle lit his dark eyes. 'I have one of your Christmas presents in Mom's apartment. Would you like to see it?'

A present? Jenny felt as gleeful as a child. 'You mean I can open it now?'

'That's why I brought it.' He gave her a teasing look that intrigued her. 'This present won't want to wait.'

Jenny and Parker slipped out of the

commons room and down the nearly empty hallways. He used his key to open his mother's apartment, and Jenny took a moment to admire the greens and bows and clever village scene that Dorothy had used to decorate the living room. It made the apartment glow with warmth. Then her eyes flew to a large basket with a red and green cushion inside it. Its contents made her eyes widen in surprise. A golden puppy with sleep in its eyes lifted its head and blinked at them. Then the dog opened its mouth and stretched, getting onto four puppy legs. A pink tongue came out and the eyes gleamed at Jenny.

'What is this?' she exclaimed. 'I didn't know your mother had a dog.'

'She doesn't. Didn't I promise you a puppy?'

'For me?' Her voice slid upward an octave, and her hands flew to her chest. 'You really got me a puppy?'

Parker's warm voice accompanied a squeeze to her waist. 'I always do what I say I will. Go on, make friends.'

Jenny fell to her knees, unmindful of the red suit she wore. As the puppy bobbed its head and came toward her, sniffing the floor and then Jenny's hand, Jenny fell in love. She picked up the dog and hugged it to her chest as the puppy wiggled and slathered kisses all over her face.

'Oh, Parker. She's adorable. What's her name?'

Parker joined her on the floor. 'That's for you to decide. She's ten weeks old, and, I might add, housebroken.'

Jenny kissed the puppy on its head and laughed and cried at the same time.

'Oh, Parker, I love her,' was all she could say. 'I'll call her Noelle, because you gave her to me at Christmastime.'

Love filled her heart, both for the man beside her and for the dog. Truly, her world was growing in a way she would never have dreamed of only weeks ago. She leaned against Parker as he gathered both dog and woman into his arms; then she set the puppy down and it rolled over, waving its paws in the air, so she could rub its stomach.

Jenny continued to babble on about how adorable the dog was and immediately made plans to take her to obedience school when she was old enough. This dog would get the best in care and training. And the residents would love her. As long as she continued to be able to work here, Jenny had to amend.

'Do you think she'll be all right if we leave her here?' she finally asked.

'Why not bring her to the show? I'll take

her outside for a walk first. She's been cooped up here for a while, and people love a puppy. You can put the basket at your feet, wherever we sit. She's still pretty young and sleeps a lot. If she does yip, I'll bring her back here.'

Jenny laughed playfully, feeling more free with her emotions than she had in weeks. No longer was she worried about the impression she would make on the corporate team. She had done her job. If they couldn't see that, it was their problem.

'Well, okay. Maybe we can take her down there for a little while. One of us will bring her back later.'

Parker fastened a leash to the red collar around the puppy's neck to take her out, and Jenny returned to the crowd getting settled for the performance.

When Parker came back in, Jenny proudly showed off her new puppy to all the residents who crowded around. Then she left Parker in charge of the dog while she checked out the seating. Some hardy souls had bundled up and taken seats outside on the upper balcony. She found Charlie, Ms. MacIntyre and Mr. Aoki there, part of the crowd. The canvas awning stretched from roof to roof and hung down behind the stage to provide a bit of shelter and keep out the wind.

For those who wanted to remain indoors, rows of chairs were set up in the library downstairs, where speakers piped in the sound from outside. And some people remained in the dining room upstairs, where the glass windows gave a view of everything that was going on.

Jenny conceded that it was an impressive arrangement.

When Grace gave the signal, the lights were lowered in all the indoor rooms, and the patio lights lit the stage. The children had taken their places on the risers, and Dorothy McAllister stepped up to the podium to begin to read the traditional Christmas story. On stage, residents costumed as Mary and Joseph mimed a conversation with the innkeeper, who pointed toward the stable painted on the backdrop. Hay had been scattered around the stage, adding to the realism.

Then the scene changed. Against a cleverly painted backdrop of hills, stars and sky, three costumed shepherds, the sheep man, one elderly resident, and one youngster, herded the sheep onto the stage. The audience murmured appreciatively, and Jenny looked more closely at the youngest shepherd, whom she recognized as her nephew.

The choir began to hum an angelic melody and Dorothy continued with her reading.

'There were some shepherds in that part of the country who were spending the night in the fields, taking care of their flocks.'

Jenny was touched with the beauty of it all and proud of them for making such a wonderful picture. After the reading, the audience was invited to sing 'The First Noel.'

She crept down the stairs to find Parker standing behind the chairs in the library. Noelle was curled in her basket, lulled by the singing. Jenny listened for a moment to Parker's melodius baritone and then shared the printed sheet with him to join in the carol. Then they sat on the stairs together, the puppy at their feet, to watch the progress of the program.

The scene changed again, and three elderly wisemen, whom she recognized as residents, led the camel on-stage, much to the delighted *oohs* and *ahs* of the audience. The readings continued as the Christmas story unfolded. Never had the story seemed more charming, all the more so because the people telling it were her own residents, people she cared about.

They were near the end of the program when some of the children from the choir crowded onto the stage that was now supposed to be the stable. Sydney was at the back of a crowd of children bearing gifts. The stage was small, and some of the players were dangerously near the edge. Then Jenny saw Roger slide off the side of the stage and creep around to the back. A warning pricked along Jenny's spine.

Suddenly, the camel, who had been placidly munching hay began to shift its large body. In its agitation, it gave an odd sort of bubbling bellow and lowered its large head to nip at Sydney, who happened to be in the way.

'Get away,' she squealed.

The audience laughed and the reader paused. But the disruption on the stage wasn't over. The camel evidently had decided it had had enough and began to stomp around. Children and shepherds pushed and shoved to get out of the way. Jenny got to her feet as the trainer, on stage as one of the players, grabbed the camel's halter. But the camel continued its screeching.

Sydney started yelling. 'He bit me. He bit me.'

Parker was on his feet in a moment, forgetting the puppy, which was roused by the commotion. As Parker started down the aisle, the puppy followed.

'Wait,' hissed Jenny, diving after the dog.

But Noelle picked up speed, yipping and wagging her tail. As she scrambled one step at a time up to the stage, she yipped at the sheep, who 'baahed' and turned their heads to stare at her.

Too late, the shepherd waved his stick to herd the sheep together. Noelle was in their midst now, yipping and nipping at their heels. One of the sheep trotted down the steps into the audience. The camel kicked out a foot, sending the kids screaming and scattering to get out of the way. The audience shrieked and laughed, and the worried staff hurried to protect the residents from animals' hooves.

As the puppy continued to slip from Jenny's grasp and wriggle under and around the sheep, Jenny's worst fears were realized.

14

The production erupted into pandemonium. Parker scooped up his daughter and moved to the side with her, calming her and inspecting the place where the camel had nipped her. He peeled off her choir robe and saw that her clothing wasn't torn. A quick inspection of her shoulder showed him no damage had been done.

He helped his mother out of the way of the milling crowd. 'Sydney's all right,' he told her. 'Nothing to worry about.'

The audience was shrieking and breaking up as the players on the stage made way for the man attempting to gather his sheep together. Parker left Sydney with his mother and turned to look for Jenny and the puppy. He saw them flash past. In her red suit, Jenny bent to grasp the dog, which barked and pranced under people's feet, under chairs and walkers.

Parker dove into a row of chairs and snatched the wriggling dog.

'I've got her,' he said.

A few feet away, Jenny leaned one hand on a chair, the other pressed to her heart. Her eyes were wide and her face was flushed. He tried to get to her, but there were several people in the way.

'It's all right,' he said to everyone.

But no one was in control anymore. Out of the corner of his eye, he saw Grace flying back and forth, trying to reassure people. Belatedly, the animal trainers took their animals off to the pens. The production was over.

Jenny retreated away from him, and he had a feeling he knew where she'd gone. Clutching the dog, he made a path through the crowd and climbed the stairs to the lobby level. He saw Jenny's red skirt disappearing around the corner, and he caught up with her just as she gained her office.

He shut the door and set the puppy down. Jenny burst into tears. He reached for her, but she twisted away and headed for the windows, crying great, noisy sobs.

'Jenny, come here, it's going to be all right.'

'No, it isn't,' she mumbled between sniffles. 'It's a disaster, and Mr. Redlin is right there to see it all. I'll lose my job over this. I knew it was too much to take on, damn it.'

Parker stood in back of her and slid his arms around her waist, pulling her into his chest and nestling his chin against her sweet-smelling chestnut hair.

'You don't know that for sure, hon,' he murmured, rocking her gently.

'Yes, I do. This place is out of control. I tried so hard, but I failed. I failed my grandmother. It's all over.'

Parker just hugged her and rocked her from side to side, letting her vent her feelings. He knew she was probably exaggerating, but he wasn't going to try to change her mind now. Better to let her cry it all out.

Her sobs lessened, but she still clutched her arms in front of her chest.

'Wait 'til I get my hands on Roger. I saw him go behind the stage. He probably goaded the camel into biting Sydney. Is she all right?'

'She's fine. She was just frightened. Her skin wasn't touched under her clothing.'

'Thank goodness for that. But she could have been hurt. That's the last time I'll let livestock in here.'

He didn't argue, just kissed her. Finally she turned around in his arms.

'Jenny, it isn't all that bad. I'm sure of it. And even if it is, we'll work it out. From now on, we'll work things out together.'

Her large, mournful eyes looked up into his, and she finally stopped crying. He handed her a tissue to blot her eyes. She sniffed and began to get herself under control again.

'That's my girl. Now, come sit down.'

Jenny sat on one of the chairs in front of her desk and gazed at Noelle, who'd curled up under the table guiltily. Jenny shook her head.

'Noelle looks like she expects us to be mad at her.'

Parker grinned. 'I know.'

'All right, girl,' Jenny said, beginning to regain some of her normal spark. 'It's obedience school for you. Beginning as soon as I can find a class.'

The dog raised her head and thumped her tail. Parker squeezed Jenny's hand.

It took some doing, but Parker finally convinced Jenny to come out and talk to everyone.

'You can't cower in here,' he advised her. 'Best thing to do is to face the music. You might find that as soon as you confront it, things won't be as bad as they seem.'

'I guess you're right,' she said grudgingly.

His heart twisted to see her struggle. And it filled him with a renewed commitment to make things right for everyone. His holiday at the Christmas tree lot was nearly over. It was time to take on the business world again so that he could make a home for the woman he loved and his daughter.

He extended a hand, the love he felt

pouring out to her. She stood up, moving closer, and tilted her head up for a kiss. Then she squared her shoulders.

He smiled. 'That's better.'

As soon as they joined the milling crowd in the commons room, people began to talk to them.

'Hilarious production,' said Mrs. O'Shay, a wide smile on her fleshy face. 'I don't remember when I've had such a good time.'

Excited children's voices punctuated the crowd as everyone told everyone else what they'd seen. Parker leaned close.

'It'll be weeks before the stories stop.'

'Yeah, maybe,' admitted Jenny.

Other residents drifted by, laughing and talking. Grace finally found them. She raised her arms in surrender.

'Sorry, boss. Apparently the camel got spooked. So much for our dry run.'

'It's not your fault, Grace,' said Jenny. 'Things just got out of control.'

'Well, at least no one was hurt. In fact' — she eyed the garrulous crowd around them — 'they seemed to have a good time.'

'I'm glad,' said Jenny.

Then her body sagged. 'I guess I'd better find the triumvirate from headquarters and face the music.'

Grace grinned. 'They're over by the

fireplace. I just passed them myself, though I don't think they knew I overheard them talking.'

'Oh?' Jenny lifted her brows. 'What did they say?'

Grace only offered a secret smile. 'Why don't you go see for yourself?'

Puzzled by Grace's sly look, Jenny made her way through the crowd. As soon as she was within speaking distance of her bosses, she apologized.

'I'm so sorry,' she said to the three executives. 'That wasn't meant to happen. Fortunately, no one was hurt.' She straightened her shoulders. 'However, I'll take full responsibility. Next time . . . ' She hesitated. *Would there be a next time?* 'It won't happen again.'

Charlie Redlin lifted his champagne glass in a salute. 'Actually, I was impressed at how quickly your staff reacted when all hell broke loose.'

'You were?'

He nodded. 'Yes, ma'am. You don't know how well-trained a staff is until an emergency strikes. Everyone cooperated to get things under control again. I think you should take credit for that.'

'I should?' She stared at him, open-mouthed.

He exchanged a smile with Mr. Aoki and Ms. MacIntyre.

'We know you weren't planning to have us here, and that put you under pressure. I just want you to know how impressed we've been with everything we've seen here. You've succeeded in turning things around, and you've created a future for Cherry Valley. No need to worry about closing your doors. If you continue running things this well, the home will keep running at top capacity.'

Jenny put a hand out to steady herself on a nearby wing chair.

'Thank you. I think I'd better sit down.'

'Can I get you a drink?' asked Charlie.

'Uh, some hot tea, please.'

Mr. Aoki went in search of a cup of tea for her while Ms. MacIntyre and Charlie sat down on the flowered sofa in front of the fireplace.

'It was a clever production,' the woman said. 'Quite quaint. You can't trust animals, of course, but as Charlie said, the important thing is that you got everyone involved.'

She smiled a wide, red-lipsticked smile and continued. 'I think the human touch is lacking in some institutions. Your residents may not be able to move as quickly as their younger friends and family, but what they really need is joy and laughter. You have provided them with that.'

'And made a profit doing it,' Charlie added. 'Your spreadsheets speak for themselves.'

Jenny was at a loss for words. She felt, rather than saw, Parker come up behind her chair, and then his hand reached down to rest on her shoulder. Ms. MacIntyre's eyes drifted up to Parker in an admiring fashion.

'The children's choir was adorable,' she told him. 'I hope they come back next year.'

'Thank you,' said Parker. 'We plan to.'

Jenny felt the squeeze of his hand on her shoulder and sagged against the back of the chair. When Mr. Aoki brought her a cup of camomile tea, she sipped it and closed her eyes. Parker had been right. It was all turning out all right.

★   ★   ★

Much later, when the party was over, Parker led Jenny outside on her balcony and pointed out a star in the sky as he stretched his other arm across her shoulders. They stood together in their warm coats.

'I told you I had something else for you,' he said.

'I can't be opening my gifts so early,' she protested. 'I haven't even bought you a gift yet. Christmas is still several days away.'

He hugged her tight. 'I know. But I wanted you to have this one now.'

He grinned at her like a kid who couldn't wait. From the depths of his coat, he pulled out a rolled-up document tied with a red ribbon. He handed it to her.

'What's this?'

Her gloved hands were clumsy, but she untied the ribbon and unrolled the heavy paper. It took a minute for her to digest the contents. When she understood what it meant, she gasped.

'Parker, how did you do this? I can't believe it.'

The document explained that she had a star named after her. Parker had written to an astronomy organization that allowed individuals to 'purchase' stars. The money went to an educational fund. Her star would go down in history as Jenny Knight. Jenny's star. She was truly stunned.

'You really meant it when you said I'd have a star.'

'That's right. I always do what I say I'll do. I wanted you to know that.'

True happiness filled her, but that wasn't all. Drawing her back inside, Parker opened a box with a winking diamond in a star setting hanging on a gold necklace.

She gasped at the brightness of it, which

almost outshone her star in the sky.

'Oh, my goodness,' she said, emotion filling her. 'It's beautiful.'

'Not as beautiful as you are,' he said lovingly as he reached around her to put the necklace on her.

Jenny's heart overflowed as she gazed at his beloved face in the flickering of their own private firelight.

'You've given me everything I could ever ask for. Beyond my wildest dreams. I don't know what to say.'

'Love is the gift of Christmas,' he whispered, just before he bent to kiss her lips.

And with love filling her heart, Jenny was no longer the grinch who would have stolen Christmas for everyone a few weeks ago. Parker had dispelled her loneliness and made her feel complete.

'Promise me you'll stay by my side,' he whispered. 'I want a future with you, Jenny Knight.'

'And I with you,' she said firmly, her hand drifting down his soft sweater as his dark eyes sought her soul. 'Whatever the future brings for us, it will be good. I know it.'

He smiled a dazzling smile as he took her into his arms. 'I know it will,' he repeated, 'because you've given me a reason to make it so.'

They spent a long time talking into the night and planning for the future. Jenny's star winked down on them from the heavens. And peace settled over the Cherry Valley Retirement Home at last.

We do hope that you have enjoyed reading this large print book.

Did you know that all of our titles are available for purchase?

We publish a wide range of high quality large print books including:
Romances, Mysteries, Classics
General Fiction
Non Fiction and Westerns

Special interest titles available in large print are:
The Little Oxford Dictionary
Music Book
Song Book
Hymn Book
Service Book

Also available from us courtesy of Oxford University Press:
Young Readers' Dictionary
(large print edition)
Young Readers' Thesaurus
(large print edition)

For further information or a free brochure, please contact us at:
Ulverscroft Large Print Books Ltd.,
The Green, Bradgate Road, Anstey,
Leicester, LE7 7FU, England.
Tel: (00 44) **0116 236 4325**
Fax: (00 44) **0116 234 0205**

Other titles published by
The House of Ulverscroft:

THE WILL

Patricia Werner

When Leigh Castle returns to the mansion she grew up in, it is not a happy occasion. Her mother has died, leaving an estate entangled by a questionable will. It is more than reason enough to rekindle the old rivalries among Leigh and her three sisters, Hania, Anastasia and Claudia. When Anastasia is discovered dead at the bottom of an abandoned mine, chilling fear takes hold of the sisters, compounded by suspicious events. But Leigh's return has also afforded her the chance to meet Braden Lancaster, the engaging young lawyer hired to handle the estate. Despite the circumstances, the attraction they feel is immediate . . .

PRAIRIE FIRE

Patricia Werner

In 1887, in the ranchlands of the Oklahoma territory, the beautiful Kathleen Calhoun is ready to start a life of her own. A chance meeting brings the handsome Raven Sky into her life. Sky is gentle and educated, but he is also a Creek Indian . . . Kathleen's attraction to Raven Sky is undeniable, but her dreams are haunted by the Indian savages who brutally murdered her parents. Torn, Kathleen flees Oklahoma and the arms of her beloved. Deep within, she knows she must return to the firm embrace of Raven Sky to feed the flames of her desire . . .

IF TRUTH BE KNOWN

Patricia Werner

Susan Franks, research director of the Association for Honesty in Government, was involved in one of its biggest cases. Law-enforcement agencies were suspected of circulating false reports on private citizens. Susan was to present her findings to a congressional subcommittee. After meeting Geoffrey Winston, she wasn't sure if they shared a dynamic attraction — or if he would use his position as a congressman to undermine the AHG: he had warned her not to dig too deeply into the matter. Susan did investigate further. When the case proved to have international ramifications, she desperately hoped Geoffrey wasn't involved . . .

I TAKE THIS MAN

Valerie Frankel

When Jersey Girl Penny Bracket is left standing at the altar by fiancé Bram Shiraz, she doesn't know how to react. Her mother, Esther, on the other hand knows exactly what to do — track Bram down, knock him unconscious with a bottle of Dom Perignon and imprison him in the attic of her mansion. Now this may seem extreme — but Esther's got some serious questions for the fugitive groom . . . plus she needs someone to write all the return labels for the wedding gifts. But can she find out why Bram got cold feet before everyone else discovers what she's done?

HEADING SOUTH

Luke Bitmead and Catherine Richards

Successful artist Cassie lives her life through her pets — her very own cast of 'Winnie the Pooh'. She's passionate about her animals — but can't help thinking she's missing out on something. That something comes in male-shaped packages . . . Good-humoured Nick, hapless and impulsive, is still reeling from being dumped by his fiancée. Thanks in part to a prank by Nick's mate — together with a black furry bundle of puppy named Rooney (after Wayne) — the lives of the two gradually come together, though neither can quite believe the reality. Can their relationship survive being plagued by ex-girlfriends, posh admirers, pets passing away and friends going into labour?